PULP Literature

I0695386

PULP Literature

PULP LITERATURE PRESS

Issue No. 47, Summer 2025

Publisher: Pulp Literature Press; Editor-in-Chief: Jennifer Landels; Senior Editor: Mel Anastasiou; Acquisitions Editor: Sierra Louie; Poetry Editors: Daniel Cowper & Emily Osborne; Copy Editor: Amanda Bidnall; Proofreader: Sierra Louie; Graphic Design: Amanda Bidnall & Sierra Louie; Cover Design: Kate Landels; Subscriptions: Carol McCauley; Advertising: Jared Schellenberg; First Readers: Amber Allen, Mark Cameron, Michaela Chan, Summer Keown, Tara King, Sylvia Leong. For advertising rates, direct inquiries to info@pulpliterature.com.

Cover painting, *Surfacing* by Jenn Ashton. Illustrations for 'Sick Pay' by Helena Pantsis. All other illustrations by Mel Anastasiou.

Pulp Literature: ISSN 2292-2164 (Print), ISSN 2292-2172 (Digital), Issue No. 47, Summer 2025.

Published quarterly by Pulp Literature Press, 21955 16 Ave, Langley, BC, Canada V2Z 1K5, pulpliterature.com, at $18.00 per copy. Annual subscription $60.00 in Canada, $80.00 in continental USA, $92.00 elsewhere. Printed in Surrey, BC, Canada, by Fraser Printers Ltd. Copyright © 2025 Pulp Literature Press. All stories and works of art copyright © 2025 their authors as per bylines.

Pulp Literature Press is based in the unceded traditional Coast Salish Territories of the Katzie, Kwantlen, Matsqui, and Semiahmoo First Nations.

Pulp Literature Press gratefully acknowledges the support of the Canada Council for the Arts and the Government of Canada.

Pulp Literature is a proud member of the Magazine Association of BC and Magazines Canada.

TABLE OF CONTENTS

FROM THE PULP LIT PULPIT

Jenn with Two Ns

In 2017, Pulp Literature Press began publishing novels, and over the course of five years we produced eight titles of which we are extremely proud: the first two Fairmount Manor Mysteries, the Allaigna's Song trilogy, the first Monument Studios Mystery, the groundbreaking science fiction novel *Advent* by Michael Kamakana, and Matthew Hughes's magnum opus *What the Wind Brings*.

However, since the release of *The Extra* and *Allaigna's Song: Chorale* in late 2022, the workload of the magazine has prevented Mel and me from developing and releasing more long-format works. This is despite having, in the pipeline and ready to go, the third Stella novel and a collection of short fiction by *Pulp Lit* author Leo X Robertson.

This is why, when award-winning author and entrepreneur extraordinaire Jennifer Sommersby posted on socials that she'd like to start a

publishing company, I asked her, "How about heading up an existing one?" She delighted us by saying yes.

Please allow us to introduce you to Jenn Sommersby, author of thirteen novels and three novellas, including award winners and bestsellers in multiple genres. Through her company SGA Books, she offers editorial services, publishing resources, and mentorship to authors. In her new role as head of novel acquisitions at Pulp Literature Press, she will be acquiring full-length novels, overseeing editorial, design, and production, and facilitating distribution and marketing.

We will be expanding our sub-imprints — which currently include mystery, fantasy, spec fic, and historical fiction — to include emotionally resonant, high-quality commercial fiction across genres. Check out our novel acquisitions page on the website: pulpliterature.com/novel-acquisitions.

And with that, we are thrilled to announce our upcoming releases for 2025: *Barhopping for Astronauts: Cosmic Horror, Late-Stage Capitalism, and Other Light Reading* by Leo X Robertson, *Stella Ryman and the Search for Thelma Hu* by Mel Anastasiou, and *Freya* by Carys Aerhart.

If the phrase *Barhopping for Astronauts* sounds familiar, we published the title story in Issue 30, Spring 2021. To whet your appetite for more fabulous short fiction from Leo, we've included another piece of his, 'Killing Time', as the feature story for this issue.

Please join us in welcoming Jenn (with two Ns) aboard to pilot this ship as it shoots for the stars!

~ *Jen Landels*

In THIS ISSUE

Cover artist **Jenn Ashton** awakens summer spirits with *Surfacing*. But where serenity resides, so too does the risk of isolation, as seen in 'Killing Time' by feature author **Leo X Robertson**.

Across time and space, the threat of silence looms in 'The Dark Mute' by **Lee Nash** and 'Frequency Eight' by **Sophie Ganic**. Meanwhile, magic and music flood the worlds of 'Waheela's Whistle' by **Scotty Olsen** and 'Their Grandfather's Chair, Part 3 by **JM Landels**.

Welcome the end along with a new beginning with 'When We Die' by **Tyner Gillies** and 'Carl's Hope' by **August van Stralen**. Then join authors **Angelique Fawns** and **MH Callway** for two difficult journeys with very different destinations in 'The Trippy Trip to Triton' and 'The Lost Diner'.

Revel in short forms with poetry by **Brian Palmu** and **Jesse Keith Butler** and flash fiction from Bumblebee winners **Cadence Mandybura, Katherine Weeks**, and **Rosanna Elves**.

At last, round out this issue with 'Let Me Tell You a Story', a new novella from **Mel Anastasiou**, and **Helena Pantsis**'s graphic short 'Sick Pay'.

KILLING TIME

Leo X Robertson

Leo X Robertson is a Scottish process engineer, writer, and filmmaker. As a writer, his work has featured in Best of British Science Fiction, Year's Best Hardcore Horror, and Flame Tree Publishing's Urban Crime anthology. His films have premiered at the Dead Northern, Horrific Hope, and ReelHeART film festivals and won awards such as Best International Feature Film and Best Smartphone Film. Most recently, he has added stand-up comedy to the list of activities he performs that inspire accusations of being an unserious, unprofessional hobbyist. In addition to being a two-time judge for our Raven Short Story Contest, he has also appeared in Pulp Literature issues 22 and 30. Find him on Instagram @leoxrobertson or check out his website: leoxrobertson.wordpress.com.

Killing Time

When Tabby closed the door on the world, she created a darkness in which something worse manifested itself. One day, it turned its key in the lock.

She was on the couch at the time, wrapped up in fusty blankets, picking at her self-cut fringe while binge-watching *DreadTech*, a show about miserable dystopian futures that brought her pleasure for reasons she didn't understand. For maximum immersion, she'd hung black blankets from the curtain poles, near-eliminating the sunlight, but square streams of it shot around the edges in white, dusty streaks.

She heard the key turning, gasped, and paused her show.

Who would dare invade her tiny sanctuary, the place she left as little as possible, where she bothered no one? Couldn't everyone do her the same courtesy and leave her alone?

The door opened to reveal a double of Tabby herself. Perhaps a better Tabby. Sleek blonde hair, immaculate eyeliner, beige mac with matching designer handbag.

The double placed the bag on a nearby armchair with a smooth and effortless gesture.

Tabby picked up a large knife from the coffee table in front of her. It had dried cheese and tomato sauce on the blade. She'd cut a pizza with it because her pizza wheel was at the bottom of the sink beneath a stack of plates.

The double paced towards Tabby. "I'm sure you have questions."

"Wh-who are you?" Tabby croaked back.

The double clasped her hands. "You hate guessing games, but indulge me, please. Who do you think I am?"

"My twin sister?"

The double shook her head.

Tabby looked to *DreadTech*, paused on the TV. "A-Are you me from the future?"

"Closer, maybe." The double grinned.

Tabby let the blankets fall off her, feeling ashamed. "Why 'closer'?"

"I can be you if you want me to." She hung up her coat and bag by the door and joined Tabby on the couch. "Think of me as your slave."

Tabby shuffled away from her.

"You haven't gone to work for two months, three days, five hours, six minutes, eleven seconds." The double smoothed her hair back. "But that's okay. I'll go in for you. You mostly hated it, and you don't have to return. Filing can be therapeutic, but you didn't find it so. It brought you pleasure only thirty-three point four eight nine percent of the time. You deserve more than that."

Tabby was speechless.

The double shuffled to the couch's other end, mirroring Tabby with a crossed knee and folded arms. "With your permission, I'll take over all your duties. I know them inside out. I've been watching you since your creation." She looked to the screen and smiled. "While you watched TV, I watched *you*." Then back to Tabby: "I'll do a better job than you and give you all the credit and benefits."

Tabby let her arms fall to her sides. "What would *I* do?"

The double grinned and held up a finger, returning to the door to retrieve something from her bag. She took out a screen and two wireless earbuds. The screen was a curved triangle shape, like it would rest perfectly on a sphere. The earbuds were angry-looking and insect-like.

"Stay here," the double said. "Entertain yourself."

"You're going to live my life while I stay here and watch Netflix."

The double's laugh was smooth and practised. "It's better than Netflix." She clicked on the screen, and it hovered before her, projecting misty white holograms.

Tabby watched, mesmerized, as images from vague dreams of hers emerged from the clouds. Elaborate castles, chisel-jawed men, the perfect outfit, Shakespearean vengeance enacted on high-school bullies. These images washed elaborate emotions over her: the sensation of having arrived, of life happening now with nowhere else to be, nothing to fix, and everyone pleased.

When the double spoke again, the images collapsed. "A stream of perfectly entertaining shows, tailored to your unique needs and desires."

Tabby half listened, irritated by the distraction.

The double walked back over to her. "These shows have a target audience of one. And they never end. There's always another episode, another series. It just goes on and on."

"Why?"

The double's face snapped to sympathy. "Haven't you been through enough? Overeducated, unappreciated, tossed aside by a world that only acknowledges you when it wants something, and barely even then." She mirrored Tabby's body language, leaning in closer after each sentence.

An obvious, manipulative ploy. But Tabby felt the words needle their way in, poking at the inextinguishable parts of her that wanted them to be true. "So you've been watching me."

"Your whole life." The double held up her front door key. "Printed this myself from the footage."

"So you saw when—"

"You were in the shower. I can provide you with that comfort myself. It would be my honour. You needn't feel alone ever again, in any capacity."

Tabby looked away and shook her head. "N-No, I—y-you saw what *happened*."

The double cocked her head.

"Two months, three days, five hours ago," Tabby said. "You're not the only one keeping track."

The double sighed. "I so badly wanted to help. You were my assignment, after all. But I was nowhere near here at the time." Her face remained flat, but tears leaked from her eyes. "It hurt me more than it did you. My species is sensitive far beyond the spectrum of human emotion." She reached for Tabby's hand.

Tabby flinched. When doubles had touched in *DreadTech*, they erupted in a matter–antimatter explosion. But when Tabby's double took her hand, all Tabby noticed was the softness of her skin.

An oxytocin rush ran through Tabby's system. Pure safety.

"The police did nothing." The double's look was hypnotic, like her eyes were expanding.

Tabby bit her lip. "It wasn't like that. I didn't describe him properly. Because of the shock. That's why they couldn't find him."

The double pointed vaguely towards the street, but kept her eyes trained on Tabby. "He lives just a few streets away. It could happen again at any time."

They stared at one another.

"It's a lot to take in." The double held the screen and earbuds out to Tabby. "Why not watch something while you think about it?"

Time lost meaning for Tabby as she lay there on the couch, bathed in the endless dopamine bliss of her self-designed shows. When she'd first put those earbuds in — whenever that was — the screen had floated up and expanded into a sphere that enveloped her head, spritzing pleasant smells and filling her field of view with constant gloss.

She spent most of her time in her favourite role, as the cool, sophisticated teen protagonist in a high-school drama set in some unnamed, affluent region of California.

All the parents had money and lived in enormous houses, so they made sure to complain as a courtesy. They never committed the transgression of enjoying a lifestyle few could afford.

All the girls at school were hot. They swarmed around Tabby and proclaimed her the hottest, which was the ultimate compliment.

All the boys had abs and infallible hair. They created endlessly epic and intricate love polygons around Tabby. Tabby with the good figure and best grades. Tabby who threw the best parties that they'd all remember forever. Tabby with the interesting and tragic backstory, which she'd learned about through tenderly treated and dreamily rendered flashbacks. The guy who did all the show's music sang with an ethereally beautiful voice, imbuing her character's longings with such striking poignancy that he simply had to be an alien. That or a masterfully designed algorithm. But Tabby tried not to think about that. Or about anything, really. She just let the sights and sounds soothe all her woes away.

Slam.

Tabby jumped up and took her earbuds out. The screen collapsed and fell into her lap, revealing her ruinous surroundings.

Dust motes clouded the air. Black fungus rotted through the walls, fluffs of white extruding from their spots. A freezer sat open by the front door, its contents thawed, water pooling on the floor, packets of vegetables wilting in the room's stale heat. Thick grime, like some weird discharge, coated the coffee table.

She couldn't say when last she'd looked around, but she'd trusted it wouldn't look like this. Why hadn't the alien cleaned?

Tabby could ask it herself: it stood there in the foyer.

"I shouldn't hear you come in!" Tabby yelled. "I don't even want to look at you."

This was her usual spiel. The alien would normally cower and mouth *I'm sorry* so as not to further offend Tabby with the sound of its speech.

This time, it scoffed at her.

"How dare you respond to me like that!" Tabby got up on her atrophied legs and walked to the door.

Something tugged on her arm. Plastic tubing ran from her vein to a drip bag that hung from a stand beside her. She gripped the stand and wheeled it with her.

"It's been weeks since you last secured a promotion for us." Her legs shook, unaccustomed to supporting her body's weight. "What have you even been doing?!"

"I just came to say goodbye."

"I don't think so. You're my slave. Or you're supposed to be." Tabby's lip curled with distaste at all this empty exertion. "You need to up the dose of sedatives in my drip. You're not changing my catheter fast enough. And we haven't made love in god knows how long."

"'Made love'. Hah!" The alien recoiled. "It nauseated me more than you could ever understand." Its laugh had a timbre like a shaken sheet of metal. "The latest reports are in. Our entertainment protocols have weakened your species to below the critical takeover threshold."

"What?" Tabby was almost in tears, desperate to defend herself—but she found her reasoning skills vastly weakened.

The alien dissolved its human hand, letting its dark feelers escape for the first time. At the sight of this, Tabby scurried to the comfort of the couch.

"We isolated you from each other." It examined its feelers with pride. "Depressed you all." It stretched the feelers behind its back, its many unseen joints popping like bubble wrap. "This was the humane option, believe it or not." It paced around the living room on newly released forelegs, which clicked on the lacquered wood. "Most declined our offer, so we ground them up for fuel. Sometimes the devices malfunctioned, which led to a suicide here and there. The rest of you we simply subdued." It turned to look at Tabby, its real eyes emerging. No cornea, iris or pupil, just two balls of pale jade. "Thank god it's over. I could hardly stand to look at you. That expression on your face as you watched your stories."

More facial features poked through the Tabby mask: dark green chitinous protuberances at bizarre angles. They were seemingly superfluous, but surely possessed functions in the alien's home environment.

"That slack-jawed face of yours," it continued, "with its dead, cow-like eyes and bitter mouth." Black feelers took over its lips, intertwining like fingers. "The more pleasure you received, the more misery it caused you." Furry antennae sprouted from its temples. "Pitiful!"

The alien tossed her coat to the floor and dropped her Tabby illusion entirely, the skin melting away to nothing. It was a slick, human-sized mantis with a wedge-shaped head. Blade-like ridges ran along its armoured shell.

Tabby howled and bunched blankets around herself. All this time, if the alien had wanted, it could have pared her out of her skin in a second.

The alien opened the front door. "It's been a blast. But I'm off to scour this stupid planet of its resources, darling." It held up a feeler. "I do have one final gift."

It tossed something that skidded across the floor.

Tabby recoiled, then gingerly peered over the edge of the couch. A round pocket mirror wobbled around. As it came to a stop, Tabby examined her bloated face, greasy hair, flaking nails. Her greying and waxy skin. 'Etiolated' was the word for it: pallid from lack of sunlight.

When had she learned that? When had she last learned *anything?*

Only the alien would know — but it had already left.

Before she could emerge from her cocoon-like dwelling, Tabby had to overcome her pre-alien agoraphobia *and* the killer withdrawal symptoms that raged through her after she pulled out the drip. Uncharacteristic waves of fury. The alien had fed her heavy opiates mixed with just enough nourishment for survival — but not a drop more.

She writhed on the floor, clawing at the wood, splinters digging beneath her nails. It was painful, but more lucid than anything she'd experienced in so long.

It was a full week before she stumbled out of the flat in her pyjamas, hungry and confused, a vice-like headache gripping her by the temples.

The air was thick and poisonous, brown smog insulating the world in an unbearable heat. It seemed to obscure the buildings and streets — but when she approached where once there had been a lamppost, a newsagent's, a bar, she discovered levelled plains grazed by amorphous black vehicles that hoovered the dust.

She backed away. A humming in the distance got louder. She turned in its direction and took slow paces ahead.

Pipes emerged from the dim. They were big shimmering metal tubes, flared at their bases where they connected seamlessly to the ground. From there, they launched high into the sky, their tributaries connecting to massive terminals that branched off higher still, through the atmosphere itself, enormous cylinders tapering out of sight. The whole network vibrated fiercely.

She steadied herself as she shuffled forwards, wondering if the pipes sucked out the planet's very core. The ground nearby buckled into depressions as big as buses, which were almost filled to the brim with corpses in tattered clothing.

"Hey."

Tabby jumped, shook, cowered.

A man, who himself looked sucked out, stood before her. Skin peeled from his face. Stringy hair fell to his shoulders. His jeans and hoodie hung from his slumped skeleton.

"D-Do I know you?" Her voice was hoarse. She hadn't spoken to anyone since the alien's departure — and not to another human in who knew how long. She could barely form sentences.

"Yeah, I'm … uh." He took her arm gently and moved them both away from the pipes' humming. "I'm the guy who mugged you."

She'd thought, if she ever saw him again, she'd recognize him immediately—but this wasn't the face that had appeared in all those nightmares. Though it did share some of the same features. The unwashed hair, the craggy wrinkles around the eyes. The scars, two ragged slices at either corner of the mouth that tore up to his ears. The divots all around them where someone—another gang member, probably—had failed to sew them up.

He wasn't afraid to share his identity for the same reason she wasn't afraid to learn it: even if they had managed to maintain scraps of their former selves, this new world obliterated their meaning.

"This is like something out of *DreadTech*," he said. "Or maybe *DreadTech*'s like something out of *this*."

She frowned. "*DreadTech*?"

"It was a TV show."

"Oh. Yeah." She rubbed her eyes. "It barely counts as one compared to what I've been watching lately."

A large metal bowl dug itself into a corpse-laden concavity, filling itself with bodies.

"Did they get you too?" she asked.

He nodded. "He looked like me. He told me he knew why I was like this. Mentioned stuff about my childhood even I'd managed to forget. He knew I wanted to change. But he said I didn't have the self-control to do it. All I'd ever known was all I'd ever know, he said. I could be no other way."

A black impenetrable monolith in morphing, non-Euclidean shapes floated along the street. Magnets selectively filtered favourite particles from the ground below. The particles rose in a fine mist, the monoliths leaving silt and dust in their wake.

The mugger continued, "My alien knew I wanted to help society. The kindest thing someone like me could do, he said, was stay indoors. He would live my life for me, better than I ever could."

More humans emerged from the remaining buildings. Most cowered in the shadows, holding their arms over their heads as if to block the sun. Some padded around in horror. All must have watched shows of their mind's design. Not only had they nothing to say to one another—unique entertainments having destroyed their once-common cultural ground—but reality clearly terrified them.

The mugger was in tears now. "We wasted so much time." He grabbed Tabby by the shoulders. "Is it like the aliens said? Is it too late to do anything?"

She went limp in his grasp, knowing he couldn't hurt her even if he wanted to. She looked back at the dust and dirty sunlight, at the indifferently humming pipes and meandering alien equipment. "I know they *want* us to think it's too late."

"But what should we do?"

She saw, in the weariness of his face, his desire to abdicate any authority, to outsource all of his thinking to her, simply because she was the nearest 'anyone else' around.

She stretched her neck, fighting off outrage. She would pretend he thought of her as important. "We can start by bearing witness." She shrugged. "It's better than what we've *been* doing."

This thought seemed to pass like a wave over others in the toxic murk. They gathered in the streets, straightened their backs, dropped their arms to their sides and stood tall.

"It's the start of something," Tabby said.

Survivors murmured to one another in loose clusters.

"It hurts to see, but at least it's real."

The mugger smiled. "We'll learn what we can. Maybe there are still actions we can take."

But as they squared their shoulders and looked once again to the street, their grins dropped.

A roaming alien vehicle passed by, using big chitinous claws to cart up bodies, both alive and dead, and toss them into an industrial shredder on its back. It crunched them with deafening volume, spraying the buildings' nub-like remains with a confetti of bloody viscera.

A ripple of survivors fell to the ground in horror as it passed by, the sight of it excruciating.

Some gripped their heads. Some screamed for the pain to end. But some got back up again.

FEATURE INTERVIEW

Leo X Robertson

Pulp Literature: *For many readers, I suspect, this story will feel uncomfortably close to home. What was one real-life observation that prompted you to write it?*

Leo X Robertson: I'm a very sensitive and antsy person, and for better or worse, I don't have the same stamina as others for TV-binging marathons. Sometimes, growing up, I'd go to friends' houses and sit watching TV for hours, and this horrible dread would creep in. I'd look over at my friends' glazed eyes and feel that something terribly wrong and irreparable had happened. Which in a sense it had, but, like, I also need to calm down, right? That's the duality of the story, haha!

PL: *Your story's conclusion takes a sharp turn into harrowing territory. (That last scene!) What motivated your decision not to pull any punches?*

LXR: It seemed logical and maximally dramatic to confront a TV-numbed populace with a real act of violence. I wanted to see how they would cope with the unsimulated reality of what had presumably entertained them for so long. But the last line is hopeful, is it not? Life can take dark paths, but if we're still around, we can always turn the tide.

PL: *In its opening, your story explains that the main character's favourite dystopian TV show, DreadTech, "brought her pleasure for reasons she* *didn't understand." For you, what is the pleasure of reading — and writing — dystopian stories like 'Killing Time'?*

LXR: Great question! Many of us can relate to the bizarre juxtaposition of living peaceful lives with mostly mild and quibbling concerns, while knowing this isn't everyone's reality. When you find yourself too invested in your own life, you need the release of remembering how much worse life is or could be. Most lives are nowhere near as bad as we could imagine. I feel there must be a reason for this. I'm a big fan of Todd Solondz's films, and he's often criticized for his pessimism. But in a few interviews he's said something like, if he can walk about on the street without being assaulted, that's a great thing. It's darkly funny, but there's also a profound truth to it. That idea motivated this story too, as you can probably tell.

PL: Writers have a reputation for being solitary, sensitive, indoor types who immerse themselves in fictional worlds for long stretches at a time. What do you do to strengthen yourself against the manipulations of an invading alien race?

LXR: Haha! Oh God. I'm afraid I have to defer to my solitary, sensitive, indoor nature in an attempt to combat this. Most of the writing I do is journaling and figuring out what I want out of life. I try to make my writing as intuitive as possible, and as a result, my intuition knows I trust it, which seems to make it louder. So if it ever flares up at something, it mostly gives me the strength to say no before I've even figured out why. Later I will figure it out, and intuition is always correct. The alien race in my story requires many yeses before they can start their invasion. Here's hoping I would say no. Although immersive VR show-streaming seems cool as hell, so who knows!

PL: *Your collection of SF short stories,* Barhopping for Astronauts, *is coming out this autumn. Can you tell us a bit about it?*

LXR: Absolutely! I'm thrilled that *Pulp* has taken this on. It collects my best sci-fi stories, if I'm not mistaken, from over five years of work. I love sci-fi when it works for me, but it can be quite an intimidating and alienating genre to try and get into. I want to offer my love of sci-fi to others, so the stories are as accessible as can be. If you think sci-fi might be for you but you aren't sure where to start, this would be a great intro. For genre veterans, there are many new ideas as well! The stories represent a spectrum of technologies and timelines, and offer as much hope as despair. If you enjoyed 'Killing Time', which you can also find in the book, you'll love the other stories too.

PL: *You're a filmmaker as well. How do you choose which medium to tell a story? Does one inform the other, and do you have a preference?*

LXR: Budget is the biggest consideration, of course. I don't think I could adapt any of my *Barhopping* stories without it looking silly, for example! My filmmaking is intensely personal and works within lots of constraints: few locations, minimal props, heavy emphasis on acting performance. So if something similar to the story happened to me, and it would be interesting enough to see acted out by just a few people in a few places, that sounds like a great challenge! If it took place across several universes and lifetimes — well, then maybe in another universe, in another lifetime, I'm out there making a film about it. As for a preference between disciplines, I live by poet James Richardson's principle that "all work is the avoidance of harder work." If writing isn't going well, I love filmmaking the best, and vice versa!

SELECT BIBLIOGRAPHY

NOVELS AND NOVELLAS

The Blood-Drenched Honeycomb (sci-fi horror), Close to the Bone
(forthcoming)
Beamed, Planet Bizarro Press (forthcoming)
Hateful Pitches (crime), Unnerving (2024)
Unfortunates (horror story collection), Unnerving (2021)

FILMS

Cherophobe (forthcoming September 2025)
Available on YouTube to watch for free:
Face Boy (2022)
Burnt Portraits (2021)

SHORT STORIES

'Lackers', in *We'll Always Be Here, an Anthology of LGBTQ+ Horror*,
Gloom House Publishing (forthcoming)
'Brief Dates with Average Gays', in *The Open Pen Anthology: Volume
Two* (forthcoming October 2025)

THEIR GRANDFATHER'S CHAIR *Part 3*

JM Landels

JM Landels *is the author of the bestselling* Allaigna's Song *trilogy as well as the spy novel* The Shepherdess, *serialized in issues of this magazine. This story, featuring Allaigna's sisters Branwen and Irdina, takes place during the events of* Allaigna's Song: Chorale. *When she's not writing, editing, or drawing, you can find Jen teaching people to swing swords and ride horses at Academie Cavallo in Langley, BC. You can find @jmlandels on most social media platforms, or at jmlandels.stiffbunnies.com.*

Their Grandfather's Chair
Part 3

Previously: Sisters Branwen and Irdina have been sent across the Clearwater Sea on a mission to soften their grandfather's heart and loosen the Mageguard web that entangles his throne. No sooner do they set foot in Rheran than they become separated when a cadre of Mageguard mistakenly arrests Branwen. Her letter of introduction exonerates her, but earns her an unasked-for escort directly to the Bastion without Irdina. Irdina is hidden from the Mageguard by the envoy sent to meet the sisters, Glaignen, and by the Leisanmira seer Nourd. While Irdina follows Glaignen through the hidden passageways of Rheran to the Bastion, Branwen is already there, awaiting an audience with her grandfather, the Prince High.

Back in the wagon, Nourd was asleep. Glaignen closed the sliding door of her bed most of the way to shelter her from the candles he lit. He no longer had her brass bowl, but he didn't need it to scry the person he knew would be waiting.

He poured a measure of water into a wooden mazer, set it between two candles on the vardo's small table, and blew on the water. The ripples danced in the candlelight and he hummed, catching the resonance till the face he envisioned began to form in the patterns.

"Irdaign," he whispered, conscious of Nourd's fitful snoring.

"Glaignen." Irdaign's voice warbled with the moving water.

He didn't reply, waiting for the woman's image to finish cohering. She was equally patient. He could see from the bundles of dried plants hanging behind her that she was in her workshop, probably looking into her silver bowl and waiting for him.

She broke the pause first, her voice clear now, as if she sat in the van with him. "Are they safe at the Bastion?"

"Yes … well. I took Irdina there by way of the spring. Branwen was escorted up the high street by Mageguard."

Irdaign swore. "Was Irdina wearing half a puzzle ring?"

"Under her glove, yes. I only saw it when she stripped down to douse herself in the spring." He lifted a placating hand at Irdaign's sudden glare. "I didn't watch, I swear. I just handed over her clothes afterwards."

"So Irdina has that much protection. And we must assume Branwen is safe, or Irdina's half of the ring would have alerted her."

"That's a powerful bit of magic you put on a girl's finger."

Irdaign nodded. "They are powerful girls, though they don't know it yet. And, like the rings, together they are nearly unstoppable."

"As long as the Mageguard don't confiscate those rings. I think, but I'm not sure, that Branwen's been marked by them. They were scouring the streets when the *Kolmond Lassie* berthed, which is why I couldn't meet the girls on the dock. But I watched from Nourd's protection. I think they arrested her first, then released her. But she went with them to the Bastion. I saw Kolluk'khan touch Branwen on the chin."

Irdaign swore again, quietly this time. "I'm going to have to hope she's smart enough to realize it and to act accordingly. As long as they can reach the Prince, I'm certain he'll allow no harm to come to his granddaughters."

Glaignen hoped that as well. Irdaign's face looked nowhere near as certain as her words.

"It's a large task you've given a pair of fourteen-year-olds," he said, his voice gentle.

"They're the only ones who could do it," she replied, a weight in her voice. "No diplomat wields more power in his heart than does a grandchild."

The stream that flowed back into the spring along the narrow stone passage was fuller than the one that led out the city's waterways. Irdina had to pick her way with care, getting her boots wet despite the pains she had taken to keep them dry thus far. After calling her grudging thanks to Glaignen for his escort through the underground paths, she turned to face the next challenge. Another waterfall confronted her, though this one at least flowed in the right direction. It was lit not by the eerie blue-greens of the cave she'd left behind, but by daylight. And silhouetted against the grey winter sky were a head and shoulders she would have recognized even if her half of the puzzle ring hadn't just warmed on her finger.

The anger in her stomach that had been building since Glaignen had put a hand on her shoulder in the market square was tempered with relief at seeing Branwen—until she recalled that Branwen had taken the straightforward route to get here.

"At fucking last," she said as she put her foot on the first iron rung stuck into the wall opposite the waterfall.

Branwen offered a hand as Irdina squeezed through the rectangular outflow, her pack getting a good soaking from the water that trickled over the edge.

"I'm glad to see you too," Branwen said, laughing in the face of her sister's curses. "Let's keep it down, though. I'm trying not to draw attention."

Irdina cursed again, but more quietly. "If you knew what I've been through to keep my shit dry. Now this …"

"Tell me all about it. But not now." Branwen looked over her shoulder at the door to the kitchens from where she'd come. As busy as everyone was in there, she had no doubt that walking through with a dripping wet sister would raise some notice. But there was another door further along the wall that separated the kitchen garden from the formal courtyard.

"Where are we?" Irdina asked, shaking the water from her pack.

"Central courtyard of the Bastion, but we're in the kitchen gardens. Our room is up there." Branwen pointed above the wall, to the second-storey windows that looked down into the courtyard.

The short winter daylight was beginning to fail, casting a gloom she felt the need to race against. She led Irdina along the path by the wall to the round-topped wooden door. If her sense of direction was correct, the formal gardens were on the other side.

"Damn," she said. There was no handle, only a keyhole. "Have you got anything useful in there?" She gestured at Irdina's pack.

"How about this?" Irdina pulled the hatpin from her green felt hat and handed it to Branwen. "I'm pretty sure I've got another in here." She crouched to rummage through her pack, which was a chaotic, overstuffed mess twice the size of the one Branwen had brought. She produced not one but two more hatpins.

Branwen had taught herself to jimmy locks at an early age, and had shared that skill with her sister. As with most of the talents they acquired, friendly competition pushed them further. Now they cooperated, Irdina holding two pins in the lock while Branwen shifted the final tumbler with the third.

The door opened with a breath of warm air and let them in, not to a winter courtyard, but to the steamy glasshouse filled with birdsong and hung with planters of out-of-season fruit and flowers.

"Great rolling bollocks," said Irdina, gazing at the lamps hung along the central roof beam to extend the short winter day. "Are those evenlamps? For plants?" There were no evenlamps in Osthegn. Their father approved of neither the expense nor the arcana they functioned with. "How much does *that* cost?"

"Wait till you see how the rest of the place is decked out," replied Branwen. "Grandpapa, it seems, has no shortage of money — or arcana."

They moved between the rows of plants towards the glass door in the middle of the long greenhouse. Irdina stopped to smell the delicate white blossoms of an orange tree in full bloom, which stood next to one laden with small golden fruit. "Look at this," she said. "Trees in two different seasons. That's not just from extra light. That's more arcana."

In addition to their father's dislike of the magic of the Colleges and the Mageguard, they had had their nurse Angeley's teachings drilled into them. Angeley quietly practised Leisanmira magic and had promised to teach Branwen and Irdina when they came of age. But the arcana used by Mageguard ... that came from deep energies within the earth and from the sky. Ones that, Angeley warned, had once caused the Cataclysm that had shaken the world and destroyed Ulaonnor-Mor far to the east.

Branwen, having been in the Bastion for the better part of the day now, merely nodded. With all the warnings Angeley had given them, they knew they were walking into a maze of wealth and power, both arcane and political. Nothing surprised Branwen anymore, and her goal was to get Irdina to their room to dry off, and then to find a safe place to talk.

In the Fox chamber that was their assigned guest room, Irdina changed out of her travelling clothes while she marvelled at the richness surrounding them. Seeing nowhere to check her hair, she reached for Branwen's cloak, which hung over the dressing table. "Is there a mirror under there?"

Branwen's hand shot out to stop her. "There is." She pulled Irdina away from the dressing table to the far side of the room, huddled close to her sister, and whispered, "But I have a feeling it's more than that. It gave me the sense of being watched. And it ... rippled."

Irdina's eyes went wide and her voice went quiet. "Watched. And listened to?"

Branwen nodded as she replied in a normal voice. "I don't think so." She made the 'lips closed' sign, and Irdina indicated understanding.

"Well, that's a relief," Irdina said with a laugh. She tapped her ear and motioned around the room. *Where?*

Branwen shrugged and signalled, *Don't know.* "You're presentable enough. Shall we go and find Grandpapa?"

After they closed the door behind them, Irdina hissed, "Why didn't you warn me there was a creepy-ass spy mirror in our room?"

"Honestly?" Branwen said, dragging Irdina along the gallery that overlooked the lowest floor. "I forgot till I got back here. I don't know that we're being listened to, either, but it seems safest to assume."

"Shit, that's a lot of magic to waste on us. Do they do this to all the guests?" Irdina whispered.

"Keep your head down and keep moving. It makes us harder to scry. I think it's me they're watching."

"Even without the mirror?"

"The head Mageguard in the group that brought me here touched my chin. It's felt funny ever since. I think I'm marked."

"Making you easier to scry. So we're just going to keep walking fast and hope they can't keep up?"

"No. I'm going to be the perfect grandchild. You'll have to be the sneaky one."

Irdina squeezed her hand—something neither of them had done since they were small. "I think I have an idea," she said beneath her breath.

Branwen squeezed back. "It'll have to wait. Put your best smile on now, and let's meet our grandfather."

The Great Hall, now busy with servants, had been transformed since Branwen first walked through it earlier in the day. Like their hall at Osthegn, there were trestle tables laid out in parallel lines that pointed towards the dais on which the high table stood. But where Osthegn's floor was covered in rushes, and more often than not sleeping hounds, the black and white chequered marble of the Bastion's floor shone bare. Instead of benches, high-backed chairs lined the tables. Those nearest the dais were wider and more cushioned, but even those at the back were polished and well-made. Of course, none of them could compare to the thrones at the centre of the high table.

"So where's Grandpapa?" asked Irdina.

"Probably in the audience chamber," replied Branwen, gesturing to the door on the far side of the hall where a few nobles loitered. "It looks like there's a queue."

An army of servants was covering the long tables with white cloths. *How busy the launderers must be,* thought Irdina as she reached down to feel the starched linen. But Branwen dragged her onward, up to the high table, which had not only a white linen covering but a runner of gold damask as well.

"This," said Branwen, standing behind the larger of the two thrones, "must be Grandpapa's." She touched the rim of the beaten-gold goblet and knew Irdina was thinking the same thing she was. *Would it be this easy?*

Irdina gave the slightest nod, pulled the vial of salts from her sleeve, and dropped a single pinkish grain into the cup. Branwen scanned the servants, none of whom paid them any heed, and then took out her own vial and dropped a pale blue grain into the cup. They were tiny — hardly visible in the shadow of the deep vessel.

"This is obviously Gwannyn's chair," said Branwen, referring to their grandfather's wife as she moved to the one next to his. "I wonder who the rest are for?"

They strolled behind the line of chairs and Irdina ticked off possibilities on her fingers. "Our aunts Perran and Miani, our uncle Phelan. Their spouses."

"Do you think their children eat here?" asked Branwen, only mildly curious.

"Just Perran has kids, and they're young. I don't see any children's seats, do you?"

"How do you keep all this family we've never met straight?"

Irdina shrugged. "I pay attention when Mother tells stories. Why don't you?" The last came out with more anger than Irdina had intended, masking the tears that would otherwise have started in her throat.

Branwen glanced at her sister, refusing to give in to emotion. "I didn't realize it would be useful."

"I didn't realize sleight of hand and lockpicking would be useful, but here we are."

"Good thing I taught you that, then," Branwen said with a tight smile. "I'll try to pay attention to the names of all our family."

"Memorize everyone else's as well. Even the servants. Do you know the name of the servant who attended you and Gwannyn before I got here?"

Branwen thought a moment. "Lallys?" she said, as they reached the end of the dais and stepped onto the floor.

"Yes, mistress?" came a voice from behind them.

Branwen turned on her heel to see Lallys set a tray full of salt cellars on the table. Branwen gave a little cough while she recovered her thoughts. "Does this ..." She waved a hand at the spread of tables. "Happen every night?"

"Oh, no," Lallys said with a bob of a curtsy. "This feast has been called to welcome you."

"That's very short notice," Irdina said. "How do you manage?"

"Our cooks are miracle workers." Lallys beamed in genuine pride.

"I'm sorry to put you to the extra work," Branwen said. "This is my sister, Irdina."

"Oh, I know, mistress." She gave another bob. "Can I get either of you anything?"

"Just an audience with the Prince," Irdina replied. "If you please."

Lallys curtsied yet again and hurried to the audience chamber door, motioning the sisters to follow.

She's not much older than we are, Irdina thought. It made her ashamed that a girl no different than they worked as a servant and curtsied to them. The staff back home were like part of the family, and their children were the friends Irdina and Branwen had grown up with.

They followed Lallys up the three steps to the audience chamber. Some of the waiting nobles looked at them with curiosity, others with annoyance. Lallys knocked.

"What?" came a gruff, irritated voice.

Lallys stuck her head inside the chamber. "The ladies Branwen and Irdina are here to see you, Your Highness." There was a pause. "Your granddaughters."

The pause was followed by a roar. "Why was I not told this earlier?"

Branwen and Irdina looked at each other, and at the vast hall set for a banquet, which he would have crossed to get to the chamber.

"Bring them in, dammit!"

Lallys opened the door fully, and a half-dozen nobles pushed away from the table in the centre of the room. Some stood, others merely appraised the newcomers.

"On your feet!" said Chanist Brandis, Prince High of Brandishear, "for my granddaughters, the ladies Irdina and Branwen of Teillai."

Technically, only their mother and father, the Duchess and Duke, could append 'Teillai' to their names, but the honorific warmed Branwen towards the grandfather she barely remembered. He, too, was standing, and was holding his arms wide in welcome. He stepped out from the table to meet them.

They began to curtsy in unison, but he swept both of them into his arms. They stiffened — also in unison.

"Forgive me, my dears. That must seem overly familiar from an old man." He stood back and appraised them, keeping a hand on one shoulder of each. "I suppose you're too grown to both fit on my knees," he said with a laugh. He waved a hand at the now-standing courtiers. "All of you are dismissed."

The nobles filed out in varying degrees of humour. As she turned to watch them leave, Branwen's eyes met the amber gaze of the Mageguard Kolluk'khan. No longer in black, the woman was dressed in workaday court attire and wore the vizier's chain of office around her shoulders. Her lips twitched in a slight smile, and Branwen felt her chin warm where Kolluk'khan had touched her. Then the mage's eyes, cold and appraising, slid to Irdina. Kolluk'khan neither bowed nor curtsied as she left the room.

But Irdina's sight was fixed on her grandfather, her childhood memories flooding back. Though she and Branwen were no longer the toddlers who had sat on his knee, his warmth still enveloped them both. She felt a pang of guilt, and the urge to run back into the great hall to dump the grains of salt from her grandfather's cup. They had only Angeley's word to go on that his mind had been ensnared by Mageguard. And how trustworthy was she? She'd lied to them all their lives, pretending to be their nurse when she was their grandmother.

Irdina's grandfather interrupted her building rage. "I'm so very sorry I wasn't able to attend Lauriana's wedding," he said. "Tell me all about it."

Branwen and Irdina glanced at one another. How had he not heard of the explosion that had killed their vizier and left their mother close to death? And, of course, postponed the wedding.

"I'm so sorry, Grandpapa," Irdina said. "We thought you knew …"

Seated on either side of him, they gave the official story. When his tears eased at last, Chanist squeezed the hands they had let him hold throughout. The squeeze felt weak, and it lacked the warmth and vigour of his earlier embrace.

"My dears," he said, "I have so many regrets." His eyes seem to be looking far away. "Lauresa … Lauresa." He looked at Irdina, released her hand, and reached across to brush the unruly curls from her face. "It's been so long since I've seen you."

Branwen met Irdina's eyes in alarm. Angeley's concerns were perhaps valid after all.

"*Irdina* has had quite the day, Grandpapa," Branwen said with deliberate clarity. "We became separated on our way here from the port, and she had to take the long route. Plus, she gets seasick."

His eyes lost their watery aspect, and he patted them each on the shoulder. "Well, I hope your stomachs settle by evening. We have a grand dinner planned in your honour. Which means we'll all need to change. Will you walk with me as far as the royal apartments?"

They left the audience chamber, one on each of his arms. As they passed through the colonnaded Great Hall and cloistered walk, he pointed out statues and paintings of their ancestors. He talked of family, those still living at the Bastion, and those long gone. He had a remarkable memory, it seemed, in all but one regard.

"Your mother," he said for the third time that day. "How is she?"

Branwen glanced behind his shoulders at Irdina, eyes widening.

"As we mentioned, Grandpapa," said Irdina with more patience and discipline than Branwen had ever heard in her sister's voice, "she seems in steady condition, but had not awakened when we left home. Angeley is caring for her."

He stopped, ran a hand over his face, and then shook his head. "Who's Angeley?" he asked.

"Our nurse," Branwen said quickly, remembering that he still did not know his first wife lived in Osthegn under an assumed name.

"I will send my physician," he said, taking them each by the arm and walking on again, "on the next ship bound for Orey."

Branwen didn't think any physician, no matter how good, would be helpful or wanted. But she kept that to herself.

When they reached the royal apartments, he opened the door and ushered them in. The page who was sitting in the upholstered chair by the fire jumped to his feet and dropped a book behind the cushion before executing his bow.

"Rhona," said the Prince, "these are my granddaughters, the ladies Irdina and Branwen. They are welcome here in the apartments at any time. My dears, Rhona has been my page for the last half-dozen years. If you need anything at all, including me, find him. And you'll usually find him here, reading cheap romances when he should be studying for his squire exam."

Rhona shrugged and gave a charming smile. "Don't knock them till you've tried them, Highness." To Branwen and Irdina he gave a second, deeper bow. "At your service, my ladies."

"Rhona, will you escort my granddaughters to their chambers and then come back to help me choose my wardrobe for tonight?" He turned to the girls. "What rooms are you in?"

"The Fox chamber," answered Branwen.

"And you?" he asked Irdina.

Branwen answered for her. "The one chamber is sufficient for us both, Grandpapa. The bed is enormous."

"Nonsense. How long are you here for? A month at least, I hope? It's not worth crossing the *Coebann* for less. Then you must have your own rooms." Neither of them mentioned that they still shared a room back home. "Rhona, make up the Swan chamber as well."

The Swan chamber was next to the royal apartments, on the first floor rather than the upper gallery.

Rhona stuck his head in and wrinkled his nose. "Been a while since he's put anyone up in here — family and most trusted only. I'll give it a dusting and freshen the sheets. Let's take you both to the Fox in the meantime."

Irdina opened the door wider to push past him. "No need," she said. "Drop me off some fresh linens. I'm perfectly capable of making a bed myself."

Branwen followed her in and stood in the centre of the room, turning slowly. The furniture was covered in drop sheets, and the carpet was rolled up against one wall. But aside from simply being unused, the room felt ... blank.

"May I escort you to the Fox chamber then, milady Branwen?" Rhona asked.

"I know the way," she replied, still distracted by the room.

"Linens?" said Irdina, pointedly.

"Of course." Rhona bowed, and then paused at the door. "If you're wondering why it feels no one is listening to you," he said, catching Branwen's eye at last, "it's because they can't. Not here." He bowed again and shut the door behind him.

Irdina looked at her sister. "What was that about?"

"Don't you feel it?"

"I don't feel anything except tired, and hungrier by the minute."

"Exactly." Branwen touched her chin, where the Mageguard's invisible mark was. "Ever since Kolluk'khan touched me, I've felt eyes. Not on me, not all the time. But I have the feeling I'm being kept track of, out of the corner of someone's gaze." She shook her head at Irdina's puzzled stare. "It doesn't make much sense, I know. But I don't feel that here."

Irdina turned to the draped lump that looked most like a dressing table and pulled the sheet from it. There was a mirror, but an old-fashioned one made of polished tin.

Branwen crossed the room in two steps and reached for it with a hesitant finger.

"Well?" Irdina asked.

"Nothing."

Irdina swore, loudly and creatively.

"What?"

"Why the fuck are we being spied on in our grandfather's home? And he knows — or suspects it — or he wouldn't have put me in this room."

Branwen looked around and felt her guts deciding to relax at last. "Because we *are* spies. And Rhona knows too."

"Which means what?"

"Grandpapa trusts him."

"And doesn't trust Gwannyn, his own wife?"

"I feel like a shit, spying on him for Angeley."

"And the salts."

"Did you see how random his memory is, though? He knows every one of our relatives and can tell us about second cousins four times removed."

"But he keeps forgetting Mama is injured." A wave of anger crossed Irdina's face again.

"The salts will help with that."

"Supposedly."

"Supposedly."

"So do we trust the grandmother we've known all our lives and who lied to us about who she was for most of that time? Or the one who put us in a room where she can spy on us?"

They fell silent, and the puzzle rings they wore tingled.

§

To be continued in Pulp Literature *Issue 48, Autumn 2025.*

For more high fantasy, family drama, and political intrigue set in the lands of the Ilmar, check out the spellbinding Allaigna's Song trilogy from JM Landels at Pulp Literature Press. pulpliterature.com/allaignas-song/

THE SOLARISTS

Jesse Keith Butler

Jesse Keith Butler is an Ottawa-based poet and the winner of the inaugural 2024 ESU Formal Verse Contest. His first book, The Living Law *(Darkly Bright Press, 2024), is available wherever books are sold. Find his poem 'Midlife Katabasis' in Pulp Literature *Issue 43, and learn more at jessekeithbutler.ca.*

The Solarists

When I got you to watch Tarkovsky's *Solaris*
for date night, and you fell asleep on the couch,
I wished I could say why I wanted to share this.
I know for you it was much too much

of the artful slow-crawl camera pans
and the thick subtitled monologues.
But for me the whole thing is how knowing ends
in the strangeness of it. See how the light fogs

the alien planetface where it rests buried
in folds of emerald ocean. That's all
I need you to witness. And, love, when we married,
it wasn't for sameness. Your tender pull

on me was this: In you I found
a mind that shone sharply apart from my bleared
awareness. When you woke that night, you groaned:
That's such a weird movie. You're so weird.

I loved you for that. And how you gave
up the next night, until the film was done.
We're adrift in the hollowed-out starlight. It's love
that holds us here, distinct and unalone.

WAHEELA'S WHISTLE

Scotty Olsen

Scotty Olsen is an Indigenous author attending UBC's MFA program for creative writing. He was selected for the inaugural Audible Indigenous Writer's Circle. He was recently published in IHRAM's quarterly literary magazine Indigenous Voices.

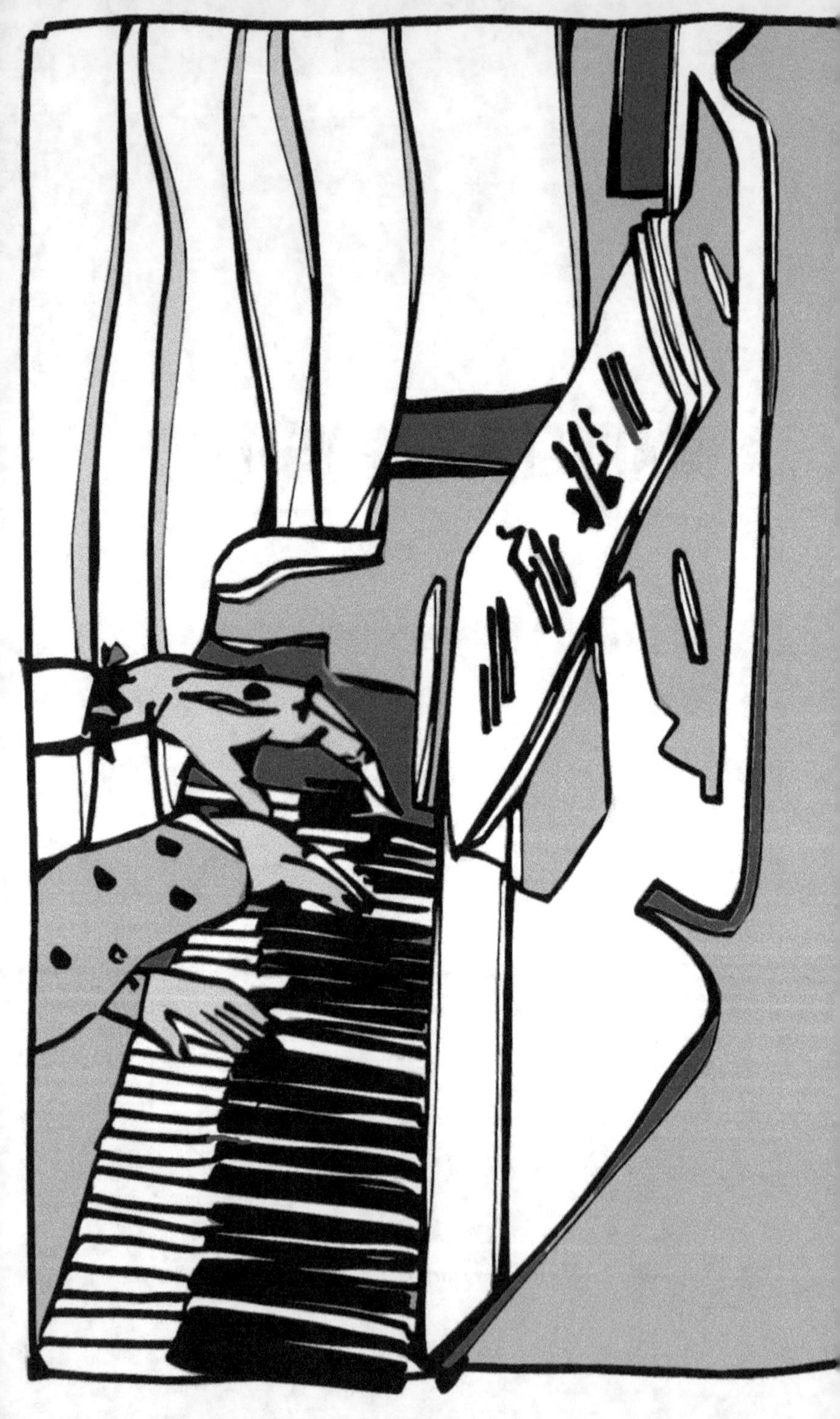

Waheela's Whistle

Kôhkom Rose had ancient hands. The backs looked like dried-out rivers. The palms were rough, wrinkled, and calloused from years of working at the corner bakery. Skin so translucent that blue veins shone vibrantly as they worked their way around the knuckles. But her strong baker's hands could still play the most beautiful keys on a piano. Sitting to her right was her grandson, a very young, blond Indigenous boy with brown almond eyes who watched carefully as the notes revealed themselves. For as long as Travis could recall, he had always sat beside Kôhkom Rose on Sundays, watching those hands dance on the keys.

"These keys are for Kimosôm," she said, her left hand stretching to the far end of the piano, "and these are for your mom." She reached around him with a smile. "This is how my mother taught me." Travis tried his best to memorize the dance those fingers performed. Much later in life, he would recall loving this part; it was their Sunday ceremony.

She smiled softly — "Pay attention" — and paused, then slowed the rhythm down to help him. She repeated the process, then grabbed his hand and placed it under hers. A warm feeling of safety swept over him as her fingers guided his. The melody she played matched the hum and the soft whisper of her voice. She pointed to each key and, aligning each syllable with a note, said softly, "Gentle, whispers, mother's, song." Each note, gently pressed, seemed to carry magic. She repeated the process, and he followed; eventually, she released her hand and placed it on his back, encouraging him to master the melody.

When he did, he looked into her olive-green eyes with the biggest smile of success. She rubbed his back and gave him a soft kiss on his forehead to reinforce his triumph. The fresh smell of lemon-scented shampoo filled his nose.

"Can you show me more … ?" he asked.

"What if I show you something truly special?" Kôhkom Rose whispered, her fingers hesitating for a moment over the keys. She then placed both hands firmly in the centre of the piano. The melody she played was well-rehearsed and carried a heavy secret. Travis felt a chill despite the warm tune, as if the notes were whispering old truths beyond his grasp.

"This music holds something special." Her hands seemed to defy the arthritic pain that had prevented her from baking, and her rhythm, tempo, and endurance surpassed Travis's comprehension. The sound made the walls vibrate; the notes found their way through the cracks in the floor and the mouse holes in the walls; loose shingles fell from the roof; and an old hearth bellowed, blowing ash into the room. The melody escaped into the avenue and brought colour to the long-dilapidated home in Edmonton's north end.

Her fingers danced at such a rapid and rhythmic pace that each corresponding note seemed to defy the sound barrier and catch up with older notes as they raced out of the home. Fallen leaves rustled, silver tin garbage bins rolled down the alleyway, and houses along Edmonton's historic 118th Avenue felt the disturbance and seemed to turn to the tune that they hadn't heard in decades. This part of the city had transformed so much over the years but still remained the same. Houses that had endured oil booms and busts, and stood when this was just a mystery of a place, the gateway to the north, turned on their foundation to watch the tune whizz by.

"Did you enjoy that?" Kôhkom Rose asked, noting his wide-eyed excitement. Travis held his response and just looked at her with a proud smile, taking it all in. Her fingers now rested as the last hammer's vibration brushed off the soundboard in the belly of the beast. The smell of dust lingered in the air as if the piano keys themselves were sweating.

She nudged him playfully, winking. "Caught all that?"

He reflected for a moment. "I did."

She chuckled. "Of course you did." She ruffled his hair. Drawing him closer, Kôhkom Rose leaned in, her voice dropping to a conspiratorial whisper. "My mom told me that melody, passed down from her mother. They said it reaches a cave deep in the mountains." Kôhkom Rose lowered and softened her whisper, her eyes alight with the magic of the tale. "It finds a crack in Turtle Island's back to sing in — and wakes up a sleeping creature.

"My mother said that if the creature enjoys the melody, it might stir the legendary beast, a massive half bear, half wolf with fur white as snow," Kôhkom Rose began, her voice becoming even lower and more reverent. "There in that cave, nestled deep within the heart of the mountain, it guards its collection of heads it has ripped off those who ventured north, driven by greed — greed for gold, oil, and our land. But it also protects our people from those who wish to take, and when it isn't protecting us, it slumbers, curled around the bodiless in the cold dark."

When she spoke, a hush fell over the room. Travis's eyes were still wide with a mix of nervous excitement and realization. He knew the cave, and the beast, but didn't tell her. His mind was filled with vivid images of the fearsome creature: two dark crimson eyes and big claws that crept out of the cave in the mountain that had visited him in his dreams. Each time, he was woken up by the sound of a whistle.

"And ..." she paused, the thick word hanging in the air. She took his hands in hers. "If the legend likes the song, it will release a sound—a melody that can protect you." Her voice softened to a whisper, compelling him to lean closer. The air between them became charged with anticipation. "And save others."

Kôhkom Rose leaned back and placed her hands back on the piano for the next lesson. "I like to think that our family's song can reach it ... and get it to release the sound."

As the last notes lingered in the warm air of Kôhkom Rose's home, they began a journey far beyond the walls that had vibrated with their rhythm. The melody, woven between generations, travelled familiar paths, riding the Pacific and wiggling its way through the Rockies until it found the right mountain. Travis grew, he changed, and Kôhkom Rose passed. Yet the notes she played that day continued their journey, a journey that stretched over years.

Kôhkom Rose's song crawls, a whisper on the wind, faltering as if exhausted and ready to give up. But it works its way closer to the cave, a place so terrifying in its mystery that even grizzly bears dared not den within its shadowy recesses. Its final form is revealed to the world as mammoth glaciers that retreat back into the north.

This mountain joins others that are forged directly along the lines of the Continental Divide, where the great waters are forced east or west. The location itself lies hidden in plain sight in the heart of the Ten Peaks Valley, just a stone's throw from the well-trodden paths within Banff National Park. Yet it remains shrouded in solitude, always finding ways to ward off anything that ventures too close. The cave is perched near the peak, on the very spine of the divide, and overlooks the valley below.

Long ago, after the glaciers left, whispers worked their way down into the valley. They made their way into oral stories about unseen forces, warnings of powers so great that they had the capacity to crack the crust, opening up the Earth with a portal to the unknown.

Echoes of tectonic plates colliding and pulling apart, of a giant asteroid hitting the Earth like a drum, of monstrous waves crashing when the whole Earth was covered with water. Sounds as old as when Theia collided with the early Earth and the debris from the impact slowly coalesced to form the Moon. Occasionally, with a wink, the ancient sentinels guarding the beautiful melodies let one escape as a gift to the Moon, who is eternally grateful to be reminded of the time it connected with the Earth.

The light of the full Moon likes to illuminate the sky and tries to take a peek inside the cave. Today, it struggles to pierce through the clouds and the evergreens that shadow it, but it manages to catch a glimpse into the cave's depths. Like a big juice jug filled with electromagnetic radiation, the Moon pours celestial juice into the thirsty core of the Earth.

If the Moon hits the spot just right, a sudden change can cause a shift and a crackle of the rocks that echoes and vibrates out of the mountain, unsettling the snow-powdered peaks of the surrounding neighbours. The trees can sense it. They turn to look. Those with only a few rings are concerned, but the ones with many rings know what is happening and place their branches on the younger ones, letting them know that it will be okay, that something special and rare is about to happen.

Then it happens. They all hear it slowly coming up the mountainside. It's Kôhkom Rose's song. It has finally reached the cave, and it works its way into its depths, guided by the moonlight.

Deeper inside the cave, a soft scratching can be heard. It awakens a massive wolf, as big as a polar bear and just as white, long believed to be a harbinger of death. From deep within, a resonant growl echoes, as if the cave itself breathes in Kôhkom Rose's song.

The older trees gesture to the younger ones to come closer. "Put your ears next to the mountain, slow your heart, and listen carefully," they say. "Yes, there it is. Can you hear it too?"

The younger trees jump back when they hear a claw scratching deep into the mixture of granite, gneiss, and schist. A high pitch, like nails on a chalkboard or a fork on a porcelain plate, echoes. Each scratch of its claw on the ancient stone sends sparks flying and magma bubbling up, as if the cave itself participates in crafting this new melody. The claw is working carefully, with laser-like precision; it's composing a message, sculpting out musical notes.

It's writing a Whistle.

Silence hovers, expectant, still.

Finger poised, time bends, awaits.

The creature concentrates on its creation.
Earth holds its breath in suspense.
Tongue out.
Then, a lift —
A pause —
A sly smile —
Melody unfolds, pure —
Revealing a primordial chime.

Waheela sorts through the pile of heads and finds the right one. It claws one from a prospector and lifts it into the air like a basketball. It presses its sharp hooks into the skull and forces its victim's eyes open, forces its mouth to read and recite the notes, still glowing like magma in the granite, and then makes the head repeat the process until it has perfected it. Paws hit the floor of the cave with a thunderous thumping as it makes its way to the opening, holding the head of the prospector. Then it extends its bear-like arm out of the cave and into the moonlight, squeezing the skull and forcing the pursed lips to release the prehistoric sound.

As the Whistle rushes out of the cave, it tumbles, twirls, and threads through, sweeping down the mountainside into the Ten Peaks Valley. The younger trees gaze in wonder, while the older ones, like parents on a Christmas morning, watch the Whistle leave them for the town. They sway gently as the last light of the Whistle's airy waltz disappears in the distance towards Banff, a small tourist town blanketed in a tapestry of twinkling lights and rich hues.

Banff is alive with the crisp scents of pines and spiced ciders, its streets echoing with the laughter of friends, families, and the festive chimes of shop bells. Crimson ribbons and golden orbs adorn the shop windows, captivating the Whistle. It approaches a windowsill slowly and sits on the ledge, taking it all in. Snowflakes gather delicately on its ethereal form, each one enhancing its shimmering presence. As it absorbs the festive colours and sounds — skates scraping on ice, couples sharing murmured secrets — it shakes off the chill and tunes into the purest pitches of joy around it.

The Whistle pauses, smiles, and then transforms into the conductor of an unseen orchestra, carefully selecting harmonies that resonate with warmth from the cacophony: a child's delighted squeal, the hearty laughter spilling from bars, and the soft whispers of reunited loved ones. It weaves these sounds into a vibrant symphony, a candy-cane mixture of melodies that encourages even distant cadences to join. It mixes all the sounds together as if creating cotton candy, and the children's laughter, friends' embraces, and families reuniting become a collective, joyous convoy eager to be part of the Whistle's grand symphony. This captures the essence of Banff's winter spirit and prompts the crowd to follow the Whistle to its next destination.

As it departs the winter festivities of Banff, the Whistle carries with it the start of its creation; each note swirls in the wind but is tethered to the Whistle in a way. As they move closer, they leave behind an echo in the valley. The journey comes to a stop at the valley beneath Turtle Mountain, where older echoes of Alberta's infamous Frank Slide reside.

Here, whispers of a century-old disaster still linger; each sound, smell, and sight is a constant reminder of the night the mountain collapsed onto the small coal town below. Buried beside the lost souls of the old mining town, the baritones from the mountain slumber with the dead. Delving into the fractures of Turtle Mountain, the Whistle wiggles and works to uncover the trapped murmurs. There, in the depths of these accidental catacombs, reside the sleeping giant baritones. With a gentle caress, a nudge, maybe a push … the Whistle awakens one such giant, its voice deep, really deep—James Earl Jones deep—a sonorous voice stirring from a long slumber. The baritone rubs its eyes and is happy that it is now its turn. It wants to wake up the others and say goodbye but knows they'll join him in the future. The Whistle takes the hand of the baritone and helps it through the layers of limestone. The baritone pauses and takes a moment to look at the Moon, a sight it has not seen in a very long time. The Whistle waits, holds its hand, until it is ready to meld its deep tones with the higher pitches hovering above. The Whistle, ever dynamic, already charts its course towards the Alberta badlands, its mission far from complete because there are more pieces to meet.

The Whistle enters the badlands high above the ground, diving down into the landscape of radiant hoodoos and layered strata, carrying the others behind it. Here lies a different history of the Earth, a history that has been etched into every colourful stripe of eroded terrain. Each layer resonates like a chord, the echoes of ancient giants seemingly trapped within the stone. It is as if the sinews of beasts that roamed these parts millions of years ago are still stretched across the land, their ancient calls preserved in the stone. The breezes here are not just air; they transform into a symphony of strings as they encounter the Whistle and its caravan of sounds. Violins, violas, cellos, and double basses seem to emanate from the sediment itself, each gust plucking at the geological layers as if they were strings on an instrument.

The Whistle plucks each sound from the confines within the rock, acting as both maestro and escort, mending and blending rich tones to join its growing chorus. The ensemble progresses, the air is filled with anticipation, the new sounds follow at a brisk pace as the Whistle hollers them over to follow closely. Moving quickly towards Calgary, past the canola and wheat fields, the Whistle continues to craft these ancient stories into the collective melody, turning the echoes of the past into the music someone needs.

The next stop is on the loneliest night in Calgary. There is no tune, no note, and no solo, just a moment where the Whistle needs to make sure that a different Indigenous boy, who is sitting on the edge of the Crowchild Bridge, has the help he needs. The Whistle explains that this isn't a part of their journey but rather another obligation. "Be patient," it explains to the others, and they wait with anticipation, eager to see why the Whistle has taken them to Calgary.

The Whistle approaches slowly along the shoreline and gestures behind for the others to keep their distance. The frigid air settles on the water as the young man exhales a deep sigh that pulls the clouds down from the heavens. He gazes down at the Bow River's shallow embrace, wondering where it all went wrong. The Whistle floats above the water for a moment, pauses, and then the moment is revealed. It spots, breaking through the surface of the water, its friend the Beaver, who lets out a faint hopeful whisper of a future yet to be composed—a future where the Whistle will need to join a different symphony. With a smile and a sense of relief, the Whistle knows it is okay to move on. It turns back and winks at its companions, and they all smile, knowing it is time to take the convoy north to Edmonton, where two final stops remain.

On the first spring day, when the warm wind joins the sunlight and melts the snow, there is a mother floating through her home. The windows are open, and all the crisp, clean white curtains dance in the wind. The air pulls lemon off the bubbles in the sink. The smell lingers as it twirls and twists in the air, then settles on the brown linoleum floor and mixes with the fresh coat of Pine-Sol. Her fingertips are pruney, her knees are dirty, her hair is up, and she smells like hard work and every cleaning product.

She is at peace. The cleaning helps her with fears and darkness. She wants to make her world beautiful for her children as they happily play outside. The chaos has been temporarily turned into order as she hums a hymn over and over.

"Create in me a clean heart, O God; and renew a right spirit within me."

That Bible verse is on an old refrigerator magnet, a reminder for her on days that aren't like today. But today, the Whistle is here to borrow the lyric from her, to siphon a small amount of happiness and weave it into the chorus of the symphony. The hymn is the bow on the gift the Whistle has been composing; the final stop is its delivery.

The Whistle escorts its friends through downtown Edmonton, looking carefully at each person on the frozen streets, at tents filled with poverty, at alleys pouring with despair, and at lives in ruin flooding the streets while others pass by without a second look. The conditions of the city's most vulnerable bring tears to the entire convoy. As they approach the core of the city, they pass city hall, the bars and restaurants, the subways, the theatres, the art galleries, and come to the entrance of the new library.

The Whistle finds a couple on a date; they have popped in to check out the new features. They spend some time playing educational games about space and talking about their own experiences on childhood field trips. Sentences are filled with 'remember this', 'did you ever do that', and 'this is my favourite'. They move next to rooms dedicated to fostering the growth and imagination of kids. They laugh and smile, trading loving looks at each other, thinking about how wonderful it would have been to have this as kids. And the Whistle follows.

They look at books they love on the shelves, and as they share their passions — their favourite authors, their favourite lines — they grow an appreciation for each other. The Whistle follows them past recording studios broadcasting songs from the street, cooking classes that fill bellies, rows of computers filled with opportunities to learn, and other interactive incentives for the public. The couple marvels at the gifts the city is providing for its citizens, especially the most vulnerable.

As the date comes to an end and they head to the exit, they hear a faint sound, a note of familiarity. One gestures to the other to follow into the hallway. The Whistle smiles. It knows what sound they are following.

He's the destination. The boy. Where a gift will be given.

The couple's curiosity leads them to the sound, which grows louder and more familiar.

"I know this sound …" one says to the other.

The couple hold each other as they come to a black grand piano located in a large opening. There is a young, tired, and homeless teenage Indigenous boy who plays the piano. His clothes are tattered, he smells of old urine, and a stick-and-poke tattoo fills his neck and runs up the side of his face. His blond hair left him years ago, around the time he lost Kôhkom Rose. Travis sits here on this cold winter, like he does every night in Edmonton, playing the notes she taught him.

A security officer consoles a patron who does not believe that type of person should be playing the piano. The couple watch and listen carefully. The couple speculate about his life. Where did he learn to play so beautifully? The internet? YouTube? An older sibling? An elder? Is he classically trained? Self-taught? They try to envision his journey, what brought him here, if he is safe, if he has a place to sleep that night, if he can stay warm. They so desperately want to know his story and if he will be okay.

The Whistle smiles at their curiosity but is more excited to give the gift to Travis. It has been all wrapped up into a symphony, every bar, every instrument, every note carefully placed. The Whistle holds it carefully while it dangles its feet over the edge of the piano. It watches Travis. The Whistle is not worried that his shoes are worn out, that he does not have a winter coat, that he has been wearing the same clothes for weeks; it knows that soon he will be all right. He is carefully playing the notes to 'Mad World', and the lyrics escape his lips so elegantly and softly that only the Whistle can hear it.

"All around me are familiar faces …"

And he dances his fingers on the F-minor keys.

"Worn-out faces …"

The Whistle watches with amazement.

The words barely escape the boy's lips, but the Whistle catches it all.

"I find it hard to take …"

The keys stop. The words stop. The couple has left. The man talking to the guard smiles with satisfaction. The security guard tells the boy that the library is closing.

The Whistle jumps down on the keys, startling Travis. Travis can see it walk up his arm. He is frozen. He looks up to see the security guard talking to him. He can't hear the words, yet he knows the motion of the lips too well. It's time to go. Travis feels the Whistle settling in his ears.

The Whistle sits and whispers to him.

It begins serenading him.

When he leaves the library, he is warm all over, even though it's frozen outside. His eyes close as a peaceful blanket comes over him.

The couple approaches him. One offers him money, the other offers their mittens and a toque, but Travis shakes his head.

They get into their car and leave.

Travis is as alone as the boy on the bridge.

He looks at the Moon, and she smiles back.

In the quiet of the closing library, Travis feels the Whistle and all its companions deep within. His voice rises like a wolf and a bear out of the womb of the world. A story comes out, resonating in the streets with fury, hope, and a beauty that transcends words. His magnanimous voice echoes a melody both haunting and healing, leaving an indelible imprint on the hearts of all who hear. And the frozen streets vibrate with the most beautiful symphony.

A sound so incredible it stops time.

Deep within the cave, the clawed creature returns to its prehistoric slumber, knowing that its Whistle has made it.

FREQUENCY EIGHT

Sophie Ganic

Sophie Ganic writes cyberpunk and dystopian stories that weave together the speculative and the profoundly human. She explores the what-ifs of technological evolution and the ways these advances can have the power to send us backwards, while drawing on themes of empathy and hope. While she's nostalgic for the science fiction greats of yesteryear, she is inspired by the relentless pace of innovation, which she uses as a catalyst for examining the relationship between our choices and their consequences. She resides in Vancouver, BC, with her cat.

FREQUENCY EIGHT

LOG OF HANNAH MEADOWS
[52°16′15.4″N 120°42′28.1″W]

September 26

I moved the plants today. I've noticed the sun is moving more slowly across the nursery. With any luck I'll be able to grow the tomatoes this year. I dream about them, the tomatoes. I move them with the sun each day. I might get a few ripe ones this season. I wish I could have fresh air, though.

"Fresh air is overrated," Joe told me once. I suspect he was trying to make me feel better.

He and Richard checked in today, as usual, but still nothing on frequency eight. I loop the broadcast every hour, hoping someone out there hears, but either my radio hasn't got the juice or there really is no one left, other than Richard and Joe, on the radio.

They get no reply to their broadcasts either. Between the three of us, our signals cover enough ground that anyone out there should hear.

September 28

Static.

I like to think about the day I heard Joe's voice crackle through my radio for the first time. He'd heard my broadcast. Serendipitous timing, nothing more, brought us together.

My message was the same with each broadcast. "My name is Hannah Meadows and I'm looking for survivors. Please respond if you hear this message."

Static.

"My name is Hannah Meadows and I'm looking for survivors. Please respond if you hear this message."

I had been trying to hear something in the grainy sound, and was about to turn my radio off for the day when it suddenly came to life.

"Hello?"

My heart pounded and my questions tumbled out like a storm. "Hello? This is Hannah Meadows. Who is this? Where are you?"

"Hello? My — Joe — lon — " The stranger's words were punctuated with the harsh buzz of the static. " — located — under my lab in — "

"Joe? Joe, can you hear me?"

"I — two years — started — "

The static whine was all I heard. I sat there clutching the microphone for a good long while.

Since that point, I haven't been alone. I have Joe.

October 5

It's raining out. Oh, to feel the rain on my face again. I never thought I would miss it so much. I spent so many years complaining about the rain and now I ache for it as if it wouldn't chill me to the core. Isn't it funny how once something is taken away, that's all you want?

"How is it raining where you are but not where I am?" Joe asked me today.

I laughed. "How can you even tell? Your bunker has no windows."

"So? I'd know if it was raining. You can smell the rain."

We still think he's about two days' walk from me.

We talked about our worst first dates. "Once, a girl told me she loved me before dessert even arrived," he laughed.

"Did you stick it out?"

"Long enough to pick up the cheque, but then I made a quick escape. I'm a gentleman but not a sucker."

Richard isn't as talkative. I don't think he has been on many dates.

October 14

Richard said today that he thinks outside air is coming into his shelter. He spent all day checking the seals but couldn't find the leak. His air purifiers are still working, and he says he has plenty of spare filters, but it's still unsettling.

From my window, I see nothing. I thought I'd see a deer, or even a bear, but I see the same trees I saw since the first day I entered my shelter.

Maybe they all killed each other too.

October 20

Still nothing on frequency eight.

"Why do you even bother broadcasting anymore?" Richard complained today. "No one is answering. We need to be out there looking for survivors."

"It's still not safe," I chided.

Joe was angry. "This virus is no joke, Richard. If Hannah thinks we should wait, maybe we should wait."

The virus. I don't like to think about it, or what it made people do to the people they loved. I think we were lucky to find our shelters, and I am *not* prepared to leave the safety of mine.

October 27

Richard has been quiet. Joe has been Joe. I'm going stir crazy. I've read the same copy of *Crime and Punishment* about six times since I've been stuck in here. Sometimes I read to Joe over the radio.

I checked all frequencies again today. I still have my loop running on frequency eight but get no response. Sometimes the static is nice to listen to, though. I like to imagine that's how the world sounds now. Fuzzy noises from wide, empty spaces. Are there any animals left?

November 1

I HAVE A TOMATO! Okay, it's a baby tomato precursor, but it's the closest I've come to actually getting a fruit. The bulb has swollen and the petals are drying up and falling off. I salivate at the thought of biting into the juicy flesh in a couple months' time.

My joy over the tomato is distracting me from the issue with Richard. He doesn't call in for days at a time, and when he does, he says little. He says his seals are fine, so that's something.

"He needs his space," Joe said reassuringly. "You know what he's like."

"He's a brooder."

"How could he not be?"

I get it. This situation is enough to drive anyone mad. We're lucky to be where we are, even if it does seem like we are the last three people on Earth. Extended periods of solitary confinement used to send people over the edge in prisons, but it's our reality. The radio is our only saviour.

We just have to give it enough time, and then maybe we can go out again. I just don't know how much *enough time* is.

November 5

Richard didn't call in today or yesterday. Joe doesn't seem that bothered by the loss of contact, but he's way more cavalier about this whole situation than I am. What if Richard is hurt? We don't really know what resources he has in his shelter beyond what he needs to live. Could he set a broken bone if he fell? If he broke his leg and couldn't move, he couldn't reach his food and water stores.

"You're worrying too much."

Joe's scolding is getting tiresome.

November 6

Still no contact from Richard. I've been on frequency eight each day, hoping that I can get through that way. Not much coming from Joe's direction either, but at least he is checking in. He knows I worry, but he's playing me off like I'm overreacting. How can you possibly overreact when the world has ended?

November 7

Joe was supposed to check in with me today. He said he'd have a surprise for me. Who knows what he meant by that? Not me, because all I heard on the radio was the same old static. I thought my days of being stood up were far, far behind me.

November 12

The radio sits silent. Richard has been gone now for a long time, and I suspect he's gone for good. I think about him lying injured on his cold, hard floor, or maybe he ran out of power and is slowly suffocating.

I have no idea why I haven't heard from Joe either. Did he go out to scavenge? He knows about the air — would he really risk that? Why wouldn't he have told me his plans?

I thought I saw a person through my window today, but it was hard to tell from so far away. I've put the broadcast loop on frequency eight again. I will sit, I will wait, and I will listen.

LOG OF JOE SCANLON
[52°3'53.6"N 121°21'51.3"W]

September 27

It's hard to remember my life before the world changed. I find myself living a twisted irony now — a virologist, perhaps one of the only survivors of a pandemic.

The lights in my lab flicker slightly, the buzz of my generator the only sound I can hear. In front of me, the mountains of papers and analyses on my desk beckon. Nothing makes sense. Hannah's voice bursts to life again through the tinny speaker of my radio. "How much data do you have?"

"Too much." I push papers aside with a sigh, but it's like hunting for a needle in a haystack. "Too much but, at the same time, not enough." I pick up a map, eyeing angry red circles that overlap each other. "Three months from the first case to the collapse."

"Symptoms?" Hannah's voice cuts in and out.

I list them off one by one. "Racing heartbeat. Insomnia. Hard to track because no one *looked* sick." It sounds so academic when I hear myself speak the words.

"And that caused people to start killing?"

"I don't know." If I close my eyes hard enough, maybe this will all go away. "We have never seen a virus like this."

The radio stays quiet for the rest of the day.

Those affected appeared normal, but it always led to one thing: murder. A kind of virally induced psychopathy? Nothing more could be determined, of course. It spread so quickly that populations were wiped out in what felt like an instant.

I don't talk to Hannah and Richard about this. They don't share the same academic curiosity. Hannah is ... the best of us. I think Richard could be the worst. But we all have our crosses to bear.

October 11

I wonder what the world looks like out there.

"Why?" Hannah asked. "What is out there for us anymore?"

I could go be with her, just her, and I would be happy.

I asked her once what celebrity she was most like. "Sigourney Weaver," she said without hesitating. "From the *Alien* movies. You?"

I laughed. "People say I look like Bradley Cooper." In my voice, she could hear my lie. In her silence, I felt her smile.

Oh, Hannah.

October 24

I don't know if I should be concerned with what Richard is doing, but he seems confident. I don't feel good about keeping this from Hannah, but so far, Richard hasn't suffered any adverse effects of being exposed to the air outside.

Richard has proposed that we team up. He argues that we have a better chance if we're all together. I don't disagree, but I want more data. I quiz him each day on his symptoms.

"I told you. Nothing." The static on the radio made his voice sound more menacing than he probably intended. "It's fine out there. *I'm* fine."

"Better safe than sorry," I said, but my heart wasn't in it.

He is winning me over.

November 6

It's getting harder and harder to talk to Hannah. I feel terrible keeping the plan from her, but there's no way she would agree, so we just have to act now and ask forgiveness later.

Richard is on his way. He should be here tomorrow. Hannah is out of her mind that he hasn't been on the radio, and I can't tell her why. I've tried to keep her calm and offer rational explanations. Is she starting to see through the ruse?

Once Richard is here safe, I'm going to tell her. I've told her I'll have a surprise for her when I next check in.

In the meantime, I loop my broadcast on frequency eight, like Hannah asked me to. It's the least I can do.

LOG OF RICHARD SULLIVAN
[52°36'36.9"N 121°42'35.9"W]

October 13

This hellscape eats at me. I'm confined to two rooms, and the seals in one are leaking. The filters are holding up, but I'm sure I've been exposed to the air by now. Hannah's calls are starting to get to me. I gave up on optimism a long time ago. Joe's all right, but I can almost see his puppy dog eyes as soon as Hannah checks in.

I don't think it's as unsafe out there as Hannah thinks it is. I'm making plans to go check. I need some supplies, anyway. I play the broadcast just to tell her I've done it, but I don't wait for the reply that will never come.

October 17

I just came back from outside. I wore my mask as a precaution but took it off when I saw wildlife out there. Birds, even a deer. If they are safe, we must be, too.

I told Joe on a private channel when I got back. "What the hell were you thinking?" I could almost see the veins popping in his forehead.

"I'm fine, aren't I? Haven't had a homicidal urge since I got back."

He didn't reply.

"Wouldn't it be better if we could all be together?" I prodded.

"Solitude has its charm," he said, but I could tell he didn't believe his own words. I can work with this. Hannah, not so much, but Joe could be talked around.

October 23

I've been out a few times since my last entry. Joe wanted to be extra sure before we told Hannah about our plan.

"She's not going to like this," he warned.

"She doesn't have to," I retorted. "Once she sees we're okay, maybe she'll loosen up. Maybe we can figure out if there's anyone else out there."

"It would be nice to have resources."

"It would be nice to have someone else to talk to aside from you two boring, lovesick assholes."

"Fuck you," he'd said, before the static told me he'd signed off, but I knew I had him.

November 4

The plan is taking shape. Joe is two and a half days' walk from me, and Hannah about two from him. I don't know the terrain but I can deal with it. My nerves are shot, but being locked up like this for two years will do that to a guy. My heart has been racing. I can feel the thumping when I try to sleep at night. Anticipation? Maybe. It rings in my ears, a constant *whoosh, whoosh*. Enough to drive a person mad.

"I'm leaving tomorrow," I told Joe yesterday. My supplies were all packed.

He paused before replying. "I'm not telling Hannah until you're here safe."

"Whatever."

The last thing I do before I leave my shelter for good is trash that damn radio. I haven't played the frequency eight broadcast in weeks. No one out there to hear it, anyway.

Joe first, then Hannah.

As I open my bunker door for the final time, the only sound I hear is my racing heart.

CARL'S HOPE

August van Stralen

August van Stralen resides in Princeton, BC. When she's not working, she enjoys walking the Kettle Valley Rail line with her wife and dreaming up stories, some of which actually get written.

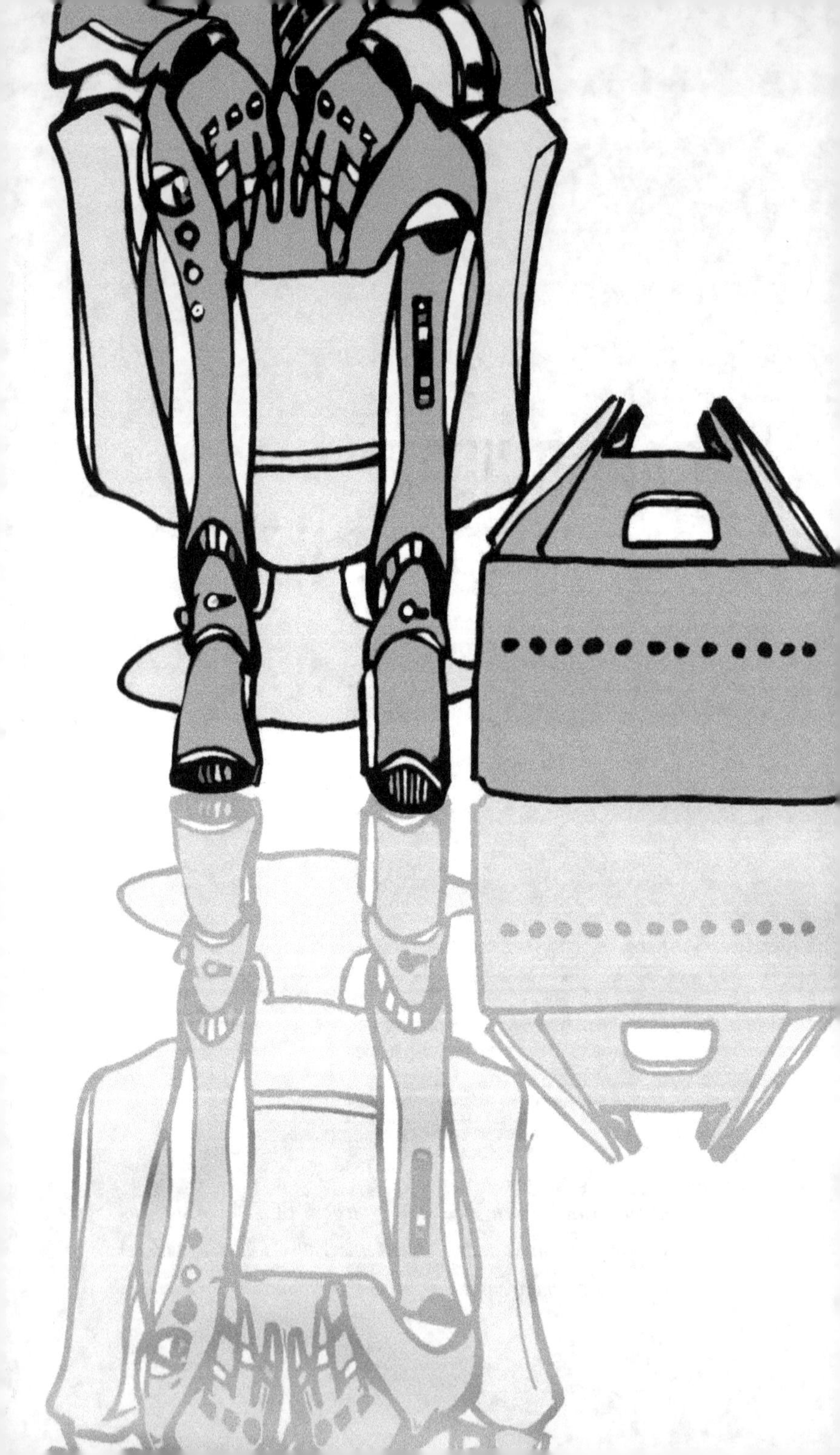

Carl's Hope

The first thing Carl did the moment he stepped out of Division Nine was turn his face to the sun. He was on mandatory emotion suppressors, but they had a side effect. They suppressed the sense of touch. Not fully, but enough to dull him to the objects around him, the clothing he wore. The sheets on his bed. But the sun … He could feel the warmth of the sun on his face and hands and any part of his body that wasn't covered. He slowly ran his hand over his hairless head. For a moment he could almost feel the calluses, the scars, the roughness of his palm.

The brace on his left leg beeped. He had been motionless for too long. In thirty seconds, he would be riveted to the spot, both legs locked until the regulators arrived and assessed his situation. If they found him loitering, they would take him back and he'd miss his one chance. Carl called up the map on his optics again and followed it to the courthouse.

Carl had expected an empty courtroom. He hadn't expected the halls and entrance to also be void of humans. Carl hadn't realized until he walked through the desolate building that he had been looking forward to interacting with people. Humans. Pure.

A small robot beeped and asked for his credentials. He placed his bald head in front of the viewscreen, almost a bow, and checked in. Cyberreception. Polite, but not engaging. He longed to hear a human voice, even a rude one. Someone to ask how he was feeling or if the weather was pleasing.

He walked to the indicated table and sat in one of the chairs. A warning beep sounded, and a moment later, his legs were locked. He would not be able to stand until released. He closed his eyes and lifted his head, remembering the feel of the sun on his face.

"Well, that's a reverent position."

The voice was female. Genetically pure. Mid-twenties. No perfume, natural soap. Natural fibres.

"Reverent position?" he said out loud. He had never heard the word *reverent* and was unable to retrieve it from his data storage. Reverent. It sounded important, somehow. He opened his eyes. The woman was as he had assessed. It saddened him, this accuracy. This ability to know so much about a person without knowing the person at all. Her shoes were hemp. Natural fibres. The only thing he imagined wrong was the colour of her hair. In his mind's eye, he had seen her as blonde, but she was brunette. It must have been the memory of the yellow light from the sun that influenced him.

"Yes, a reverent position. Face turned up to the sky." She stopped in front of him. "I'm Compass Lew. I will be representing you in court today." She held out her hand. Carl stared at her. Humans didn't usually touch his kind, at least not willingly. He hesitated only a moment before reaching out with his own hand. The movement was slow, controlled. He wanted to believe he controlled his movements but knew that, while in the presence of the genetically pure, all his mechanical components were controlled by the Command Centre. But he believed that if he had been permitted to decide, he still would have chosen to move slowly, to keep his grip light in her hand.

He smiled at her. Though his facial expressions were his own, it felt forced. "Pleased to meet you. What is *reverent?*"

She sat down beside him and placed a small tablet in front of her.

"Belief in God or a higher power." She looked at him, eyebrows knitted. "You weren't programmed with a god, were you?"

"I was not. What is a god?"

She turned back to the tablet, flicked through some of the screens, then tapped it once. An image of Section Nine appeared on the wall in front of them.

"A god is a higher power, a being, that guides us, humans, through life. They forgive our sins and, in exchange, we give them reverence."

"What kind of sins?" He could not find this reference in his data storage.

"All of them. Theft, lying." She stopped talking for a moment and looked at him. She seemed to be studying him. "Murder. Killing."

Carl looked down. His clothing hid the design of his body, but the outline of his enhancements could be seen through the fabric. And some of his mechanics couldn't be hidden by clothing. The circuitry on his bald head, the one glowing eye. Blending in wasn't an option for his kind. Section Nine segregated him and others like him from the rest of society. The genetically pure did not want to see him, to be reminded.

"I have sins," Carl said. He could sense her watching him. He knew she was studying him, and he let her. There was a bang as the courtroom door slammed open. Compass Lew jumped. Carl touched his hand to hers and held it until her pulse slowed. He wanted to ask her about why they were here, about his case. About Hope. But he hesitated. Two guards, their thick-soled boots striking the floor, marched loudly to the front of the room. They kept their hands in the pockets of their vests. Sentries. Non-genetically pure. They could be painlessly disabled by injecting the tap at the base of the skull with nitrogen. Carl had disabled hundreds. But he wasn't here to fight, at least not in that way.

One of the guards raised his voice. "All rise. Lady Magistrate."

The locks on Carl's legs beeped, and he was moved to a standing position. Lew stood as well. A woman, in her mid-fifties, marched into the room from a door to the left of the courtroom. Her heels clicked on the white stone floor, adding an echoing tap to the swoosh of her robe. Wool. Unusual. Thick. Organic.

She took the chair behind the box, protected now from everyone in the courtroom. From Carl. "You may be seated."

The mechanics in Carl's body forced him to sit again.

The magistrate looked down from her elevated bench. "Compass Lew, you represent Unit 2275?"

Lew stood up and bowed slightly. "Yes, Your Magistrate. I am representing the Unit in this matter." She looked at her tablet, flipped through some screens, but did not say anything else.

"Unit 2275, please stand." The magistrate didn't look at Carl as she spoke. He was moved to a standing position.

"My first instinct—my human instinct," she said, fixing her eyes on Carl, "is to deny your request and walk out of this courtroom. And there would be few who would stop me." Her eyes flicked to Lew then back to Carl. He could see the magistrate's heart rate was elevated, but she wasn't afraid. This was anger and determination. He had sensed it before. It hadn't stopped him.

"Please explain to me why you believe your case should be heard."

Carl opened his mouth to speak, but Lew spoke first. "Carl has been living in Section Nine for" — she glanced down at her tablet — "seven and a half years. During that time, he hasn't been involved in a single conflict and has been a model citizen of the Compound."

"Display his profile," the magistrate said to the guard on her left. He touched a device on the box, and an eight-foot colour image of Carl in full assassin dress was displayed on the wall to Carl's right. Carl didn't recognize himself. It had been almost a decade since he'd worn the carbon-fibre suit, the steel boots, the black helmet. The gloves had prevented him from ever feeling what his hands were doing.

Height: 189 cm. Weight: 91 kg. Kills: 163. Name: Unit 2275. Designation: Supreme assassin.

"Supreme assassin," Lady Magistrate said. "One hundred and sixty-three kills."

Carl looked down at his hands, palms open. Under the scars, he could see the wires and veins, the markers that kept him from being neither fully cybernetic nor fully human.

"He has paid for his crimes," Lew defended, but her voice was not strong. Carl wondered if she believed his punishment was enough to pay for his crimes. His payment had been constant monitoring. The leg locks, the hand locks, the pills that kept him from feeling. The desolation of the Compound — or the graveyard, as the other Organetics called it. It's where they put his kind after the wars were over. More humane than death, they said, but it wasn't living. They were supposed to serve as a reminder of what humanity had done, a warning to never let it happen again.

"Tell me, Unit 2275—Carl." The magistrate seemed to spit his name like dirt from her mouth. "What was your designation during the wars?"

Carl was raised to a standing position again. The algorithm controlling his body knew the rules of human interaction better than he did. He blinked at the magistrate and swallowed. "Butcher," he replied.

"Butcher." She leaned forward, arms resting on the box. "And why did they call you Butcher?"

"I didn't just kill. I dismembered." He had been trained not just to kill, but to frighten survivors. The body parts had been delivered to others as warnings. "Did you enjoy dismembering your victims?"

Carl shook his head. "I did not feel pleasure, only a sense of accomplishment. I had completed the task to which I had been assigned, within the parameters that had been defined. It was what I was trained to do."

Lady Magistrate sat back. "Is it still what you are trained to do?"

"No. The program still exists, but it has been suppressed. It is no longer at the forefront of my consciousness."

"Lady Magistrate," Lew interrupted. "This is my first Organetics case, and I was very reluctant to take it." She glanced at Carl then turned back to the magistrate. "My entire family was wiped out by Organetics during the racial cleanse. "But this changed my mind. May I play a video for you?"

The magistrate seemed to consider Lew's request. Her nod was slight, but Carl noticed. Lew seemed to notice as well, but only after a moment of heavy silence.

"Thank you." She tapped her tablet again. Carl's image disappeared and was replaced with a video of him in his room. He was lying on his bed, back to the room, one hand moving up and down in a stroking manner, but the angle prevented the viewer from seeing what he was touching.

Carl watched, transfixed, wishing and fearing the camera would move, or he would move, so his dog would be displayed.

"This is Carl with the dog, though in this video you can't see the dog. He was very good at hiding the animal."

Carl turned his focus to the magistrate. Her heart rate and her facial expression were still hard.

"The organic sensors in the section can only detect living beings of more than three kilograms. The dog was just a puppy when Carl found it," Lew said. "He was able to conceal the dog from the sensors for at least three months before anyone was aware a genetically pure was in the section."

The magistrate narrowed her eyes. "You concealed the puppy from the sensors?"

Carl nodded. "I knew if discovered, Hope would be taken away."

The magistrate furrowed her brow. "What did you call it?"

"Hope."

"Why do you call it that?"

Carl dropped his head for a moment. Sucking in a breath, he looked first at Lew then Lady Magistrate. "She came to me when I had no hope. She needed me. I had a choice: feed her or let her die. I believed if I turned her in, she would be destroyed."

"Why would this dog's death matter? You're a killer."

"Not anymore," Carl replied.

"But that's a result of your programming. You said yourself that the killer program has been suppressed, but it's still there."

Carl ignored the tone of disbelief in the magistrate's voice. "She touched me when no other living thing would. She sought me out. I did try to let her go, when she was bigger. I left the door of my complex open, but she would not leave. And then I realized I could not leave her.

"I searched historical records," he continued. "There was no record of an Organetic ever having a dog. But there was no record that stated an Organetic could not have a dog. I knew if they found her, she would be taken away. I found the adoption request form and filled it out."

"Do you really think you have the capacity to care for a dog?"

"Carl has been caring for this animal for seven months," Lew responded. "He fed her, bathed her, kept her safe. The puppy stage is always the hardest. It's the greatest test of any parent." She looked at Carl, pressed her hand down on his. He could feel the warmth of her fingers.

The magistrate's face remained hard. "What are your intentions with the dog?"

"To meet her needs and give her the best life she can have."

"And if that best life is with a genetically pure? What then?"

Carl's voice broke as he spoke. The pills kept his emotions in check, but somehow the misery, the sadness, of losing Hope shot through. "Then I must allow her that best life."

"Lady Magistrate, if I may?"

The magistrate turned to Lew.

"I would like to bring Hope into the courtroom."

"This is highly irregular, but I will allow it. I would like to see the Organetic with the animal."

Carl held his breath. He could hear his blood pumping, his heart rate increasing as the seconds passed. When the door finally opened, he gasped. Hope tugged at her lead, eyes fixed on Carl. The handler released the catch, and the dog raced to Carl. He scooped her up and laughed as she licked his face. He could feel her tongue, the warmth of her breath, the softness of her fur.

"Enough." Lady Magistrate smacked a gavel on the box. Carl snapped to attention and focused on her. Her heart rate was elevated, but her features were soft.

"Adoption granted. Trial basis only. You will be monitored. The dog will be fitted with a life collar. Anything happens to the dog, you will be destroyed. No trial."

"Agreed. Agreed with all my heart."

The magistrate hit a button, and new orders appeared in Carl's optical processor. He saw the words *guardian. Protector.* Hope was now truly and legally his. Carl nuzzled his face against Hope's fur, hiding the wave of relief that washed over him and made him want to cry. He kissed his dog then turned back to Lew. He wanted to thank her for saving his life, for saving Hope. He hadn't chosen to be a killer, to be the Butcher. But he had chosen Hope, and she had chosen him.

"Compass Lew," he said, "I think I understand reverence now."

ALAGOAS FOLIAGE-GLEANER

Brian Palmu

Brian Palmu is a poet and critic currently living in Victoria, BC. His two poetry chapbooks are Sunset Mathematics (Frog Hollow Press, 2017) and Parade (Anstruther Press, 2024).

Alagoas Foliage-Gleaner

Not dominating the pale grasses
like the black rhino, nor dramatic
like a sprung jaguar, the bird vanished
before a forest of veiny sky.

Losers hunt by foot, waiting endlessly.
Air conditioning on, in a bower
of pixels, you're free to download and hear
brief jagged rattlings of the gleaner.

Stuff that tiny black eye under a thumbnail.
Bird thou once wert, and where you twitched and sang
an excavator Cat now prowls and rattles
late afternoons.

THE DARK MUTE

Lee Nash

Lee Nash writes poetry, fiction, and creative non-fiction. Her work has been widely published and anthologized (Brink, Magma, Southword, and The Best Small Fictions 2019) and has won or placed in international competitions such as the Bath Flash Fiction Award, the TU Dublin Short Story Competition, and the Bridport Prize. You can find her at leenashwriting.com.

The Dark Mute

I take it into my mouth and swallow, nervous the cotton
will give. The button holds fast, its hard disk pressed snugly
into my lips. There's enough space under the stiff papier-
mâché mould to breathe and, despite my apprehensions, I
don't feel claustrophobic.

The velvet is delicate, its nap as smooth as a panther's muzzle.

I clench my mask at the beach — no need to sport a sunhat
or pollute the seawater with chemical lotions. My age spots fade.

It protects me at dinner parties. The hosts waft their haute
cuisine past my fashioned nose and replace my cutlery clean and
dry. The perfect guest, my opinion unrequired, I find myself
frequently invited. The bourgeoisie waves me from château to
opulent residence as I pocket their patronymic names and digest
their conversations about the Society of Jesus, the intake of
seminarians, and the Bordeaux commuter belt.

At mass, I spit out my bead to receive the Eucharist, fitting it
back like a baby's dummy. The priest tilts his head and squints
at my non-face; I don't flinch.

I slip it in place for the psychologist. This session, I won't regurgitate my toxic trauma; she has no reason to apologize for her insensitivity and doodles in her notebook.

It serves me well in shops, except when *gendarmes* arrest me in banks and escort me from *boulangeries*. Incognito, I'm charged and fined with a bevy of sculpted ladies dressed in zentai suits.

No one can see me cry or smile, or tell if my soul is mourning or dancing.

Eclipsed, invisible, mute, I engage people rarely — if I'm so inclined.

Others follow my lead and cover their features. Tyros prop their shades over the eyeholes, pierce their fake philtrum or paint lip liner on their false vermilion border. Newsreaders record their voice-overs in advance and dress as patricians.

Far from disempowerment, we begin to heal, manage our stress, and regain our centre.

My mock interview goes viral. Yes, I nod, I was the first woman to wear the moretta in public. Yes, I applaud its revival from the seventeenth century. The media fills my blanks and writes itself a cheque.

Our motives being veiled, a suspicious mob surmises all manner of objectives. We could work against the general interest. No, we shake our heads: we represent the oppressed and harassed whose voices are silenced. From a peevish angle, our new seductive weapon undermines the unisex cause.

We have nothing to disclose. Behind our bathroom doors, we remove our visors and catch ourselves in the mirror, grinning, each visage an infinite Guy Fawkes.

Partners and lovers come home. They beg to stroke our flushed cheeks but we suck resolutely on our buttons. *Later*, we gesture wildly, while writing the audit or setting the omelette.

If deprived of company, we wrap our disguises in silk and relax our embouchures, alone.

Emboldened, we grab our daughters by their slim wrists and join hands with femmes in flash mobs, naked apart from our camouflage. Uninhibited, our silent chant ascends to heaven.

There are rumours of insurrection. The inner life is deemed communal property; human intentions must be plain and visible. We carry poison between our tongues and our teeth.

I'm on trial—snagged by a legal technicality. It's a crime to hide your physiognomy, to decline to speak when you're spoken to. The Church comes out: my God-given gifts are meant to be shared, offers the curate. The state won't bail me out: I've incited rebellions and strikes and domestic violence, it rules.

Stripped of my *servetta muta*, my screen of mystery, I collapse. Not guilty, I plead.

In my cell, there are no buttons on my prison clothes. There is neither black cloth nor thread. If I refuse to communicate, they deprive me of my privileges. If I shield my face with my blanket, I go to sleep cold.

In time, of which there is plenty inside, I make a decision. Even without my façade, I have the element of surprise.

I stutter and progressively talk. There is now so much to say. I sing till my captors are weary and release me from my cage. With words, music, and wise women, I rebuild my world.

THE TRIPPY TRIP TO TRITON

Angelique Fawns

Angelique Fawns is a journalist and speculative fiction writer. She began her career writing articles about naked cave dwellers in Tenerife, Canary Islands. After selling her first story to EQMM, she fell in love with weird fiction, which is actually stranger than non-fiction. She has had over a hundred stories published. Find some in Mystery Tribune, Amazing Stories, and Space & Time. You can find her lurking @angeliquefawns on X, blogging about upcoming calls at angeliquemfawns.substack.com, or gazing into the abyss, hoping it stares back at her.

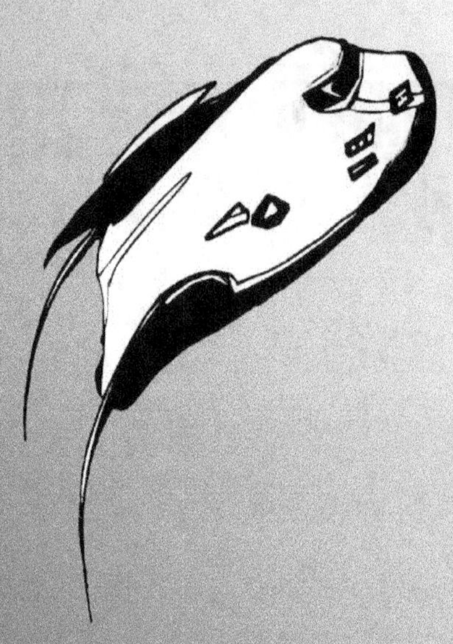

The Trippy Trip to Triton

Angela couldn't keep her eyes off the box-shaped bulge in the back pocket of Liam's designer jeans. His magnetic Radus gravity boots were kicking up sidewalk dust, he was walking so quickly. Her stomach was doing somersaults as she rubbed her sweaty palms on her thrift store skirt. Was he finally going to ask her?

He looked over his shoulder and gave her a toothy grin. "Babe, you're gonna love this! It's the trip of a lifetime."

Perspiration trickled down her arms, more from nerves than the hot Texas weather. Her feet were sore in her own gravity boots, a gift from Liam. The smell of jet fuel and the heavy perfume of the flowering magnolia trees nauseated her.

Her head still throbbed from their private party last night. Molly and mojitos. In her neighbourhood, it was easy to find drugs. That was how she'd attracted the great Liam Dawkin in the first place. Short skirts and street narcotics.

"I don't know ..." She trailed off.

He gestured expansively at the looming glass entrance of the Dawkin Houston Centre of Space Science. "There are benefits to being a Dawkin! This is the first so-called tourist flight to Triton ever. It's just you and me, hot stuff."

She wrinkled her nose in a way she knew he found adorable. "How on Earth did you get a private flight?"

He shrugged, his broad shoulders pulling his golf shirt tight. "When your family funds the whole dang program ..."

She tuned him out. Liam had probably eaten a custom omelette created by his family's private chef before he picked her up. She'd had stale cereal. Not that she'd been able to choke down much breakfast. Her tongue was a sand dune, and panic dusted her gut.

"I've never even been on a plane." She hated the whiny tone creeping into her voice. "I don't like heights."

He winked at her and rubbed under his nose. "There's nothing better than getting high!" His nostrils were red at the edges.

She bit her bottom lip. "It's just that my family couldn't even afford trips to the shore—"

He interrupted her with a wave of his hand, his champion football ring glinting. "Those days are over. One day you'll be Mrs Dawkin, and we'll take one of our private jets to any beach on or off this world!"

She blushed. It was time to put on her big-girl panties and conquer her fear of flying. If that was an engagement ring in his pocket, not only would her future be set, but her mom could stop working three jobs.

Bile clawed up her throat like a cat on fire. She gulped it down, wishing she'd thought to pack antacid. But Liam had told her to pack nothing—they'd buy everything at the Triton bio-habitat. She tried to let his enthusiasm infect her, but fright was a strong vaccine against fun.

A drummer beat on her forehead, the opening act to a huge headache.

The thought of a romantic proposal on Triton's icy surface kept her from fleeing. She'd seen videos of first explorers floating in low gravity. Maybe that's why he bought them both magnetic boots. He planned to get down on one knee under the blue glow of the enormous Neptune moon.

The visual calmed her as if she'd popped one of Liam's Valiums. The drummer took a break.

She smiled as he jogged ahead of her, much the same way he led his college team onto the football field. Huffing to keep up, she concentrated on his perfectly sculpted behind. The bump on his bum was the right size to be an engagement ring. The sharp edges of whatever he was hiding was whitening the denim. Would it be a ginormous diamond? Or maybe one made from the rare metal they were mining from Triton's core?

They entered the towering building, and the cavernous lobby was empty except for one security guard. The guard nodded at Liam. Angela took deep breaths of the lemony cool air, but her blood pressure rose the closer they got to the launch pad.

The HSS *Nirvana* was the first spaceship of its kind. She gulped as she studied the long, lean bullet, its hull casting an ominous shadow. That cat was back in her throat, its fiery fur blocking her airways with panic.

She took a deep, shuddering breath and focused on the unbelievability of it all. Look how far she'd come in life since that stinky rent-controlled unit on the wrong side of the air tracks. Angela Smith was going to be one of the first tourists on Triton!

She might even return home engaged. Her shoulders relaxed, and acid went back to her belly where it belonged. Angela rubbed her hands together, visualizing a sparkling jewel on her left hand. The thought of it made her dizzy, like the first time she'd winked at Liam and offered him a taste of her special gummies. Her cheeks went red with the memory. That wasn't the only sweet thing he'd sampled that night.

It had been surprisingly romantic. The two of them had climbed one of the towers over the commuter air railway and gotten high. He'd pointed to the stars and told her he'd take her up there one day. The memory stirred up butterflies in her belly. She'd told him she was a "terra firma kinda girl" and wanted to stay right there on Earth. Why couldn't he propose to her on their special railway tower?

Angela poked him in the ribs. "How did I let you talk me into this again?"

Liam was tense with excitement, his fingers twitching. "We do this right, and it will be the ultimate trip. I heard my father warning his research team about it. A side effect of wormhole travel is intense euphoria."

The anxious cat of acid crawled back up her throat. She swallowed and tried not to puke. Of course, Liam had found a way to make this about getting high. Cocaine to help him on the football field. Pot to help him relax after a game. Ecstasy to improve their sex life.

Angela crossed her arms over her chest. "Your father is worried people will get addicted to space travel?"

Liam laughed. "They knock you out for the flight. You don't get to experience any of it." He lifted one side of his mouth. "But we will."

A shiver ran down her spine. "That's why we're here? So you can try a new kind of high?"

"Yup. But for every high, there is a low." Liam pulled the box out of his back pocket.

Angela's heart leaped. He was going to do this now? Right before they got on the ship? Her hands flew to her chest. It was a beautiful box, painted with little leaves—

The little leaves were marijuana plants. Disappointment washed away her adrenaline.

He flipped the lid and showed her a row of pills. "I got my painkillers and downers right here. Hangover prevention."

Tears welled up in her eyes. Pills. Not a ring.

Angela sighed, trying not to let her devastation show. "So what's the plan here?" She'd have to keep playing the fun party girl for a little longer.

Liam pointed to a blue vein in his arm. "It's easy. When they hook you up to a tranquilizer bag, slip out the needle right after the technician leaves."

"Are you sure it's safe?"

Liam nodded. "Someone must have done the trip awake, or how else would they know?"

Angela frowned. "I'm not sure that qualifies as a scientific—"

Her boyfriend, on a roll, ignored her. "Two trips in one! Not only will we see Triton, the largest moon of Neptune, but we will trip out and expand our minds." He flapped his hands by the side of his head like little wings.

For a moment she hated him, her eyes rolling as she scowled. She caught herself before he noticed and smoothed her brow into the expectant ingénue look she knew he liked.

She could fix her face, but autonomic responses were a little harder. Angela's nose twitched when she noticed the smell of her own sweat, acrid and only partially masked by vanilla deodorant.

Her plans were plummeting out of her control.

She didn't want her mind expanded; she wanted to get married. Craning her neck, she looked up into the blue Texan sky through the launch aperture. She searched for trip-cancelling clouds. Sometimes spring in Texas could bring freak storms. Instead, the sun shone brightly.

She tucked her cheek onto Liam's bicep. "There's got to be a reason they knock you out for the trip." Being cute sometimes helped her get her way.

Liam was oblivious, jittering with excitement. "Nah, it's like opioids. Too good for everyone."

Angela chewed on her lip. "Why do we have to get high? You can have a good time sober."

"No, you can't." Liam laughed and gave her a quick kiss.

As always, her stomach flipped when his dry lips brushed hers. Even frustrated with him, she was still infatuated with him.

A white technician opened the shuttle door. "Okay, Liam. Time to load you and your plus-one."

Angela's anxiety flared like fourth of July fireworks. It was happening. She gave a small gasp and put her hands on her knees, fighting off a full panic attack. Liam grabbed her hand and raised his eyebrows. Those blue eyes, that aquiline nose, the entitled set to his chin. She wanted to be a part of his world. No matter what the cost.

She forced her trembling legs to move, and Liam hauled her onto the ship that smelled like a new car. The HSS *Nirvana* was fresh off the lot, with travel pods that looked like metal coffins. Tubes snaked from pink fluid bags beside each one. A high-tech hearse.

Angela wrenched her hand back. "I'm not sure I want to do this."

Liam frowned, an ugly frown. One she only saw the few times she defied him. "If you back out on this, you're backing out on me. I'm not adventuring through life alone."

"What do you mean by that?" She hated the quiver in her voice. It was the little girl's voice she'd had when she was caught stealing an apple from the cafeteria in third grade. The one that begged you not to be mad at her.

He gave her one of his less pleasant smiles. "You want to be Mrs Dawkin one day, don't you? Push your boundaries!"

Her cheeks flushed with the familiar panic she felt whenever he threatened to break up with her. She was more afraid of losing him than frying her brain. How stupid was that? She balled her fists. It was also stupid to be poor your whole life.

She kissed his hand. "I'm sorry. I love you, okay? If you want to push boundaries, so do I." A wave of self-hatred filled her throat with bile.

The anger faded out of his blue eyes, and his trademark grin split his face. "Ready for our excellent adventure?"

She gulped, shuddering a bit at the vile taste, and looked at the travel tubes. Definitely coffins.

The technician hooked up her IV. "You're aware of the risks?"

Angela gave a final desperate look at Liam. His eyes were gleaming with excitement.

"Yes." Her brain frizzed with panic.

Squeezing her eyes shut, she thought about picnics on the Dawkin Estate lawn, a designer dress floating around her vacation-tanned legs as she sipped on champagne. That was her future.

She hardly felt the pinch as the needle slipped into her vein, and her eyes fluttered open. She glanced to her left and Liam gave her a thumbs-up.

The dream champagne popped and disappeared. The lid of the coffin closed over her.

She was trapped.

Sweat dripped down her forehead as the cabin dimmed.

This was the moment of decision.

She could pull the IV out and get high with Liam. Or she could play it safe and black out for the trip. But Liam might dump her if he discovered she chickened out. Her fingers touched the metal needle in her arm as her breath came in short, harsh gasps.

The drummer returned and beat on her temples.

Do I really need Liam to make a good life for myself?

What if he dumps me anyway and I have to find my own way? Go back to school?

She would need her brain. It was too risky to travel through a wormhole and fry every synapse. Who needed a man so badly that they'd risk their intellect?

Angela laid her arms down on the plush grey cushion and left the IV in place. She was at peace with her decision, and the drummer took a break. The rumble of the ship getting ready for blast-off rattled her bones. The drug in the IV set in with a heavy languor as she closed her lids to blackness.

Bang Bang Bang

Angela jumped when a metallic smacking shook her tube. She sucked in the cold, stale air and tried to see what was hitting her tube. A film of vapour prevented her from seeing anything out of her coffin window.

Bang Bang Bang

Angela slapped at the release button, and the lid creaked open.

An apparition of terror leaned into her pod. Angela screamed and jumped out on the other side.

"Annnnngela," the creature croaked.

Her eyes widened at the old, wrinkled man. She recognized the blue eyes, even if they swam in a sea of red. It was Liam. Age spots marred a bald skull. His tanned skin was impossibly wrinkled and pale.

He cackled with swollen gums. "You missed it, babe! Was that ever a trip!" His strange titter dissolved into a hacking cough.

Angela fought the scream crawling up her throat. "Liam? Are you okay?" It came out as a shriek. She knew it was a ridiculous question. Obviously, he wasn't okay.

The skinny, liver-spotted man fell onto his bony bum. The butt that had once been firm and perfect. His coughing escalated, and she realized he was laughing again.

Liam clapped his gnarled hands. "I got high, all right. Turns out you bend space and time, it just keeps bending. Bend and bend and bend." His words were mushy without teeth.

Angela fought revulsion and reached one hand for him.

Shivers of hot and cold ran through her as relief warred with regret.

Relief that she kept the IV in her arm for the flight.

Regret that she hadn't stopped her boyfriend from going through the wormhole awake. Not that he ever listened to her when his mind was set.

Regret that her dream of a perfect life with a gorgeous, young husband was gone.

Liam rocked back and forth. "That was a rush, all right. The trip to Triton was trippy. I tripped and tripped."

His eyes rolled up into his skull, and he hit his temple with his football championship ring. The sound made Angela wince. She reached over and stilled his arm, slipping off his ring. It came off easily, his fingers skinny now.

"Don't hit yourself, love." A sob caught in her throat.

She stared at the heavy ring, the green topaz catching the light from the control panels. She slipped it on her left hand.

Liam moaned, and she stroked his bald head, the skin papery and thin. He quieted.

Her brain ticked furiously. The drummer in her head picked up his sticks and started a slow *tap tap tap*.

Only she knew his box contained pills and not a ring.

What if he had *proposed to me on the gangplank?*

She would be a hero, the woman who wouldn't leave her brain-damaged fiancé.

We could get married right here on Triton.

Full drumroll. She had a solution!

She kissed Liam's withered cheek. "Babe, you wanna get married? Today?"

He clapped his veiny hands and cackled. "Yes, yes, yes." A shiver wracked his body. "That was some trippy trip!"

Angela smiled at him sadly. "It sure was. The trip of a lifetime."

THE LOST DINER

MH Callway

MH Callway *is an award-winning author of short crime fiction and the thriller* Windigo Fire. *She has published two collections of her works:* Glow Grass *and* Snake Oil. *She and Donna Carrick are co-founders of the Mesdames and Messieurs of Mayhem, a national collective of 25 leading Canadian crime writers. They have published six anthologies, including the 2025 Derringer finalist* The 13th Letter.

The Lost Diner

At night, the road changes. The pavement becomes an endless grey ribbon spooling out between dark canyon walls. Iridescent road signs leap out like startled deer, houses sweep by like lost islands.

When I was a kid, I'd stretch out on the back seat of my dad's Studebaker and imagine we were driving along the bottom of the sea. Wind-tossed trees became seaweed; oncoming cars were deep-sea fish on the prowl. The vibrations of the road beneath me spoke of drowned crevasses, monsters, and the abyss.

Funny, the things you remember. Especially after driving solo for hours and much of that time in the dark.

Didn't help that I was driving blind.

Ten hours ago, when I'd left Toronto, Marco, Reese Motors' night manager, stopped me. Leaning his pudgy arm on the roof of the BMW MX 8, he'd said through my open driver's window, "Terry, I know Reese and Mike backed you for this run, but, I gotta admit, I got problems."

"Right. I'm a woman. Worse, I'm old."

"Hey, you said it, not me."

"Good thing the boss man, Reese, likes my driving." After all, Reese made twice as much money on my runs because he paid me half of what he paid his boys.

"Oh yeah? 'Cause Mr Reese says this is your last chance. You gotta be faster." He pulled out his phone, scrolling with a thick finger to find his notes. "You got the customs documents for the BMW? Your passport?"

"Yes, Mom."

"Look, I'm just doing my job here. OK, the drop-off is Lexington, Kentucky, the Starbucks parking lot on 9 2 2."

"The Starbucks next to ABS Auto Repair," I broke in. "Leave the BMW at Starbucks. Keys go in the auto shop's drop box."

"Yeah, and no cell phone, no toll roads, and no stopping. We clear?"

"As crystal. Can I say goodbye to my kid now?"

While we'd been talking, Mike — the tall, well-built guy who'd once been my baby — had turned off his welding torch and strolled over from the wreck he was restoring.

"Hey, Mom." He crouched down next to the driver's side by the open window. "Big run to the US of A tonight. You OK?"

"First Marco, now you." I poked his bare forearm. "Hey, is that snake tat new?"

"What, you don't like it?" He exchanged man-to-man glances with Marco, who sniggered. "You're crossing over at Lewiston, right?"

"Lewiston's slower," Marco put in.

"Bye, Mom." Mike leaned in through my open window and kissed my cheek. And slipped something into my hand. I felt his grip tighten on my fist to stop me looking at it.

"I'm not a fan of that tat," I said.

"You're wasting time here," Marco said.

I stomped down on the gas pedal and rocketed out of there. But Mike had scared me. His dark eyes had that look, the one he always got fighting off bad childhood dreams.

At the first red light, I got a look at what Mike had palmed me: a note wrapped around a key.

The note said, *Valuzilla Storage, I-90, number 89.* Guess that's why he'd stood up to Marco about my crossing the border at Lewiston.

Luck was with me. I made it through customs in twenty minutes with no problems. Probably the chilly wet November weather helped chase traffic away.

Despite the rain, Valuzilla Storage was easy to find. Its pulsating green neon sign showed Godzilla stomping on a heap of storage crates. Hardly the best ad to reassure customers about the safety of their stored property.

The place itself was deserted. It was one of those single-storeyed outside facilities like rows of garages stuck together. Number 89 lay halfway down the centre row.

The key Mike had slipped me worked. At first, when I rolled up the outside metal door, the unit looked empty. But as my eyes adjusted to the dark, I spotted a cardboard box against the wall.

Back in the safety of the car, I opened it. On top was a brown paper envelope and underneath it, a cell phone—and a gun. A Glock 17, fully loaded. Inside the envelope I found a set of paper maps and a note from Mike that said: "Call me when you get to Buffalo."

I shoved the Glock under the driver's seat and headed south on I-90, questions pinballing through my mind. What had

Mike gotten himself into? He'd landed me the job at Reese Motors because I'd worked repo for the insurance company. From the start, I'd figured Reese Motors was shady, but I stayed on, didn't look at stuff I wasn't supposed to see, and never asked questions.

I needed my job. I needed to keep my son safe.

At a drive-through Dunkin Donuts in Buffalo, I called Mike's cell number. He answered on the first ring. "Hey, babe."

He must still have been at work. "It's me. What's going on?"

"Nothing's going on, I swear."

"I, um, got everything you sent me. This is a burner phone, right?"

"That would be right," he replied cheerfully. "We still on track for tonight, babe?"

"Yeah, we're good. Ahead of schedule, actually."

"Great. Stay in touch." He rang off.

Worry ate away at me, but for now, I'd stick with the plan: deliver the high-end BMW — and whatever Reese and Marco had hidden inside it — to Lexington, Kentucky, by 5 a.m.

I drove on.

At a quick and dirty gas station break between Cleveland and Columbus, the first icy fingers of fatigue sneaked into me. Marco and the boys could drive twenty-four hours at a stretch through any weather, stoked up on nothing but testosterone and caffeine-laced drinks. Lately, driving nights, almost nothing could stop my eyes from closing, my mind drifting into dreams …

I switched on the car's radio and found a raunchy rock station. Who can sleep when Steve Tyler's scream-singing "Walk This Way"? That helped for a while.

Just past Columbus, though, a human voice broke through the stream of retro rock. Major accident on I-71: truck rollover, multiple cars involved. Four-hour delay minimum. No way I'd make Lexington by 5 a.m.

I took the next exit ramp, pulled over at the lonely service station there, and studied the paper maps Mike had given me. Looked like I could use county roads to detour around the accident, though it meant veering east, deep into the back country.

I called Mike, explained the situation.

"I don't like it," he said at last. "Weatherman's calling for severe thunderstorms down south. Out in the country, with poor visibility, you could mess up. On the interstate, it's safer."

"And I'll miss the drop-off."

"I'll deal with it. Stay on the interstate, like I said. Stay in touch."

Forget it. If I missed the drop-off, Reese wouldn't only fire me. He'd take it out on Mike.

I decided to risk the detour.

Ten miles down the road, the storm hit. The trees by the side of the road tossed like seaweed in the BMW's high beams. The sky cracked open in a burst of blue-white light, and the threatened thunder-shower sluiced down over my windshield like a firehose. Even the BMW's pricey windshield wipers couldn't keep up.

The narrow country road had no shoulder: I couldn't pull over. And it was too dark to stop on the road itself: some local boy might come roaring up behind me and smash me into oblivion.

Water cascaded over the road. Grabbed at my wheels. I felt a flash of nerves. The BMW was hydroplaning.

Nothing to do but slow to a crawl and steer in a straight line. And pray the road ran straight, too.

In the distance, I spotted a faint yellow light perched up high. A street light? A gas station? A row of lit-up windows materialized through the driving rain, like a phantom vessel lost on a storm-tossed sea.

I turned toward the lights, my hearing deadened by the rain battering down on the car's roof. Gravel crunched under my tires. The BMW bumped and lurched over uneven ground.

My headlights struggled through the downpour. Rain danced in brown potholes all around me: I'd landed in an unpaved parking lot.

A blue neon sign flickered above the windows: Mother's Diner. Through the rain, light glinted off a metal grille on the other side of the lot. An F-150 pickup had parked next to the lamp-post. Looked like the diner was still serving.

I let out a long breath and switched off the BMW's engine. OK. I'd take a few minutes, wait out the storm. And I desperately needed coffee.

I grabbed my phone to call Mike. No signal. I slipped it into my jeans.

I turned on the BMW's security system, grabbed its electronic key, and cracked open the driver's door.

Always be safe, that's what my dad had taught me.

I reached under the driver's seat for the Glock. Shoved it into the inside pocket of my black leather jacket and dived into the storm.

By the time I reached the wooden steps leading up to the diner's door, my jeans and runners were soaked. I pushed my way inside. Stood there dripping over the black and white linoleum tiles.

For a moment, I felt like I'd stepped into the old diner where my dad used to take me as a kid. He'd treat me to a strawberry milkshake if I shut up while he and his cronies did business.

A low counter with steel-rimmed stools stretched in front of a pass-through into the kitchen. Booths with red vinyl banquettes lined the windows. In the one at the far end, two men sat hunched together, deep in conversation—the only other customers.

At the cash, beside a glass display case holding a solitary pie, stood a heavy-set woman about my age. Her thick auburn hair clashed with her pink-and-white waitress uniform.

I nodded to her and slid into the booth nearest the door. From there I had a clear view of the BMW through the rain-splattered window. My weathered reflection stared back at me: my long grey hair in a braid down my back, my sunken dark eyes …

"Coffee?" The waitress had shuffled over to my table. Not waiting for my answer, she plunked down a thick white mug and filled it from a glass coffee-pot. "Creamer and sugar's beside you."

The coffee smelled like road tar. I'd need a front-end loader of that chemical sand she called 'creamer' to whiten it. One sip and I'd probably stroke out; my blood pressure was already in the red zone from agonizing about Mike and keeping the BMW on the road. But, hey, caffeine is caffeine.

"Thanks." I took a sip and tried not to pull a face. I reached for the plastic menu propped up by an old-time glass sugar dispenser with a steel lid.

"Kitchen's closed. Sorry, hon."

"OK, how about a slice of that pie?"

"I wouldn't. It's kinda old." She glanced back at the two men. "I could make you some toast instead."

"Sure, that'd be great."

She trudged back behind the counter. As if on cue, the two men at the back stood up. Young wolves, both of them: one bald, one blond. Blondie grinned at me, teeth showing.

For a heartbeat, I feared they were headed my way. That my sixty-two years made me a target instead of acting like my precious cloak of invisibility. But when they reached the cash, they shoved past the waitress and disappeared through the swing door into the kitchen. A moment later, laughter and a murmur of voices drifted from the pass-through. Sounded like the wolves and the cook out back were buddies.

I fingered my coffee cup. Had I made a mistake stopping here?

The waitress was back. She set down a plate of buttered toast in front of me. Factory-made white bread, the kind I grew up on.

"You travelling by yourself?" She handed me a plastic packet of grape jelly.

"You always work nights?" I said, answering her question with a question. It was a trick my dad had taught me. An old cop's trick. A sergeant on the police force till the day he died, did I mention that? More bendy than bent, but a cop always.

She shrugged. "Got no choice. When Jimmy out back says jump, I jump."

"I hear you. Working women our age get no say."

"No kidding." She stared at the kitchen. "Mind if I join you?" She set down the mug of coffee she'd poured for herself.

"Sure, that'd be nice." I bit into a slice of toast.

She settled down on the bench opposite me. "My name's Gilda-Rose, by the way. Gilda, like the old Rita Hayworth movie." She smiled.

Looking past her pale, sagging features, I could trace her fine bone structure. Her eyes were a deep blue. One time, she must've been a knock-out.

"I'm Terry," I said, opening the grape jelly.

"Nice to meet you." She groped in her apron pocket, pulled out a crumpled pack of cigarettes, and offered me one.

"No thanks, but you go ahead." I'd quit smoking twenty-five years before when I was expecting Mike.

She lit her cigarette with a gold-plated lighter. An old-fashioned job with a quilted metal pattern down the sides, an ST Dupont lighter like my dad's. An odd, masculine thing for her to have.

"Nice car you've got," she said, inhaling deeply.

"It's not mine. I'm just the driver."

"I see. Who does it belong to?" Her eyes shone with curiosity.

"Some old lady," I said, sticking closely enough to the truth. On paper, the BMW *did* belong to Marco's mother in Miami. "She owns a condo down in Florida. Likes to use her own car down there."

She blew out a long plume of smoke. "Bit early for snowbirds, isn't it?"

I shrugged. "Like you said, when the boss man says jump, I jump." Time to change the subject. "What about you, Gilda-Rose? How did you end up waiting tables in a diner in the middle of nowhere?"

"Oh, Jimmy and me … Well, it's a long story." She arched an eyebrow. "I was hoping you'd say that I look familiar somehow. Ask me if I was ever in show business."

"Well, I'm not big into movies, but you colour your hair auburn like Rita Hayworth. And you're a good-looking woman."

"Flattery, I love it."

I grabbed another slice of toast. "Is that where you got your lighter? From your showbiz days?"

"Why're you asking?"

"It's pretty valuable. You're working a crummy low-wage job, yet you still keep it. It means a lot to you. Or the guy it belonged to did."

She twirled the lighter on the table. "How much do you know about Hollywood?"

"Not much."

"You're lucky." She drew a small metal flask from her apron. "Want some?"

I shook my head. "Better not, I'm driving."

"Don't drink, don't smoke. You're a real straight arrow, aren't you?"

"Hardly."

She smiled, dosed her coffee, and took a deep, nourishing swallow. "The biz runs on who you know, surprise, surprise. When I first landed in Hollywood, I didn't know anybody. I grabbed this gig in a singing diner, where I belted out show tunes, hoping to get noticed. This old guy, Otto, was my regular. Mr Eggs-on-Rye-Toast." She dosed her coffee again. "One day, he asked me to the movies. A bit weird, him being forty years older than me, but I was alone and broke. Why not, right?"

"Right."

"He took me to see this old war picture. He held my hand in the dark, but that's all he wanted. Romance." She looked wistful, remembering. "And, you know, the movie wasn't half bad. Afterwards he told me he'd directed it."

"Sure," I said.

"I know, that's what I was thinking, too," she said. "But there was his name, right there in the credits. Thirty years before, everyone — the studios, the critics — had said he was going places. I don't know why he never made it. He should have." She threw me a crooked smile. "That's showbiz. You gotta love it."

Guess who the lighter once belonged to.

"Why was your friend, Otto, still hanging around Hollywood?" I asked.

"Oh, he never stopped making films. They were his life. He slid down into B pictures, then bad indie stuff, then real garbage. Guess you know what kind of films I'm talking about."

Porno, the dark mirror world of Hollywood that no one acknowledged. With, obviously, an unlimited number of wannabes to draw on for 'talent'.

"You'd be surprised how many big stars started out in porn," she went on.

"No, I wouldn't, I guess. Did you … make films with Otto?"

"He tried to talk me out of it. But that was my way into the biz. I wanted in more than my life." She flicked Otto's lighter, fired up another smoke. "I wanted to be extraordinary."

I looked out the window. The rain was still coming down hard. "So what happened?"

"Oh, eventually, Otto let me into the business. He always looked out for me. He even asked me to marry him."

"And did you?"

She burned down half her cigarette before replying. "Yes, but he died. Lung cancer."

"I'm sorry."

"Hey, listen to me, doing all the talking," she said. "What's your story, Terry?"

Tell them nothing, always stay safe. I finished my coffee and scraped up the last bits of grape jelly with a crust of toast.

"I drive cars. That's what I've always done," I said.

"But now you're your boss's slave."

I forced out a laugh. "It's complicated. My son …" I barely stopped myself in time.

"*He* got you the job, huh? How does he like working with his mom?"

"He doesn't." I stared at the dregs in my coffee cup. "Like I said, it's complicated. Do you have kids?"

She looked away. "No, it never worked out for me."

"How'd you end up here?"

"Things got tough after Otto died. I never made it, was never meant to make it. Jimmy was working the pictures, too. We hooked up, travelled the roads for a bit, then washed up here at his mom's diner. When she died, we took it over."

"You and Jimmy are partners."

"Yeah, real romantic." She stubbed out her cigarette on my now-empty plate. "Jimmy only treats people one way."

"Why don't you leave?"

She shrugged. "Like you said, it's complicated."

I no longer heard voices in the kitchen. Outside the wind had picked up. A dark figure was standing next to the BMW. Water streamed off his leather jacket. His soaked hair shone white under the spotlight. Blondie.

I stood up.

"Something wrong?" she asked.

"Yeah, that guy's messing with my car."

She twisted round to look out the window. "Oh, that's just Duane. He's harmless. He and his brother Reilly are big into cars. They run a body shop up the road."

Chop shop, more likely. Duane caught me staring at him

through the window. He flashed me his predator's grin before he sauntered over to the pickup and climbed in the passenger side. Reilly, the bald one, was driving.

The pickup churned out of the parking lot and swung onto the highway, heading deeper into the backwoods.

I dropped a ten-dollar bill on the table. "Thanks, for the coffee and toast, Gilda."

"Forget it," she said. "It's on the house."

"Then you keep it."

"Wait!" Her hand gripped my wrist. She looked at the kitchen, lowered her voice. "When you leave, head for the interstate."

I smelled him before I saw him behind the counter: a queasy mix of cooking oil, sweat, and alcohol. Jimmy, the cook, was a balding, fiftyish man wearing a grey T-shirt and sweatpants. He'd probably grown those ropy arm muscles pumping jailhouse weights — and learned to cook there, too.

"Why aren't you working, Gilda?" He came round the counter.

"Come on, Jimmy. Nobody's gonna show up in this rain," she said.

"You're still on the clock. This oughta cover it." He snatched my ten-dollar bill off the table.

"I gave that to her, not to you," I said.

"Nobody asked you." He shoved his finger in my face. "Stay out of this."

"I'm giving Gilda a ride," I said. "She's leaving with me."

"Is that right? Well, she owes me." He scooped up Otto's lighter. "This oughta cover it."

"Give me that back!" Gilda scrambled out of the booth, but he held it out of her reach.

"Give her back the lighter!" I said.

His small blue eyes flashed when he saw my gun. I could almost hear the neurons in his lizard brain clicking over, weighing how to take me out.

"How about you hand over your keys to the Beemer?" he said.

Too late, I saw the hunting knife in his other hand.

I felt a rush of air. Gilda swung the sugar holder. Crunched against his temple. He cried out, fell on his knees.

He twisted like a snake. And plunged the blade into her thigh.

She screamed, and brought the sugar container down on his skull. Something broke loose inside her. She hammered down on him in a frenzy.

"Stop, Gilda! He's had enough. Stop!"

I shoved the gun into my jacket. Tried to pull her off.

Suddenly she sagged against me. The sugar container fell from her fingers and rolled away under the counter.

"I'm sorry, Jimmy. I'm sorry." She burst into sobs. "Is he … is he dead?"

He sure didn't look good, lying there, staring up at nothing. My breath was coming in bursts, my heart was churning. I tried to focus.

"Gilda, you're hurt. Help me now. I need to see where he cut you. Try to stand up."

She was a big woman. Though I'm a fair height and fit from the gym, it took nearly all my strength to heave her onto the nearest stool by the counter.

Jimmy's knife was still lodged in her thigh. Before I could stop her, she seized the handle and yanked it out in a gush of blood.

Must stop the bleeding.

I stumbled over to the cash and found two tea towels under the counter. Her wound was deep, blood welling up like crimson oil. I knotted the towels together and wound them round her thigh in a tourniquet to staunch the flow. I prayed it would work.

"I-I'm cold." She was trembling all over.

"You're in shock. You're losing blood. I'm taking you to a hospital."

"No! No hospital! They'll call the cops. Ask questions."

"It was self-defence. You saved my life."

She shook her head. "You don't understand. Jimmy's done bad stuff. A lot of bad stuff."

She stared at the knife in her fist. "This was his favourite. A Bushcraft Special. Best thing for hunting, he told me."

I uncurled her fingers from its handle, one by one. Dumped the knife on the counter. "Leave it." I had to get her outside into my car. "Try to stand up. Lean on me."

"No … pointless." She looked up at me, her eyes full of tears. "You can't carry me, Terry. I'm too heavy. We both know that. Can you … can you please get me back my lighter?"

Steeling myself, I kneeled down next to Jimmy's still form and pulled Otto's keepsake from his limp fingers. When I handed it over, she pressed it to her heart.

She groped in her apron for her cigarettes. Her hands were shaking so badly I had to hold them steady to help her light up.

She took a deep drag. "Please go before Duane and Reilly get back."

The young wolves, the not-so-harmless locals.

"I heard Duane say they were getting an amp back at the shop."

That figured. They'd need a power amplifier to bypass the BMW's security system. Breaking in the old-fashioned way would scratch its paint.

"I can't leave you. What'll those two do to you when they find Jimmy?" I asked.

"Nothing."

"I don't believe you."

"Please, Terry, just go."

She was giving me a free pass. I'd be a fool not to take it. And I had to think of Mike.

I opened the diner door and stepped onto the porch. Outside there was nothing but darkness and relentless rain. The spotlight shone down on a sea of mud; the blue flickers of Mother's neon sign danced in the deep puddles.

I hesitated, the chill rain soaking into me. I was back in my childhood nightmare, lost at the bottom of the sea, my feet sinking into the sediment of the abyss. That's when I saw a point of light in the void, racing down the highway: the deep-sea hunter out for prey.

The wolves were back.

I rushed back inside. Gilda sat where I'd left her, huddled by the counter.

"Jimmy's buds just showed up." I fumbled for the door's bolt lock and turned it. "Where's the light switch? We're lit up like a movie screen in here."

She pointed behind the cash. I scrambled over and killed the lights, plunging us into semi-darkness. The outside spotlight continued to shine down on the parking lot. It was on a different circuit.

I swore. "Quick, let's hide in the kitchen."

"I can't … the pain."

"Look, if we're stupid lucky, they'll go for the BMW, give up, and leave. They won't check out the diner."

"But the power amp?"

"My boss fixed its security system. Power amps won't work."

Through the window, I watched the pickup roll into the parking lot. "Please, Gilda. We have to move."

"OK, I'll try." Through the murky light, I watched her push down on the counter with both hands and lever herself up.

"Come on, you're doing great," I said.

She draped her arm over my shoulders. Bracing myself, I managed to take her weight. Together, we half-staggered, half-fell through the swing door into the kitchen.

I took a deep breath, willing my night vision to kick in faster. An open grill and stove stretched halfway down the kitchen's back wall. The door at the end was our only other way out. Its outside lamp was still on, another source of dim light.

Midway between the grill and the pass-through lurked the shadowy form of a prep table. Judging by the rank smell of leftover food, it was littered with dirty pans and dishes. I steered us over to it.

The banshee cry of a siren pierced the night. Lights strobed over the parking lot.

"Cops!" she gasped.

"No, it's the BMW's security system. Told you the amp wouldn't work."

Thumps on the front porch, the grind of the front door handle.

"Hey, Jimmy, you in there?" a man shouted. "Come on, dude, open up!"

"That's Duane," Gilda whispered to me.

"Hey, you got her car keys? Come on, man, turn off the damn alarm!"

Gilda let out a moan and glided down to the floor, legs splayed. "That noise, it's driving me crazy. Can't you do something?"

I crouched down beside her. "If I turn off the alarm, they'll know for sure we're in here."

"And when they go round the back, they'll see Jimmy's van. They'll know he never left."

Fair enough. "Has Jimmy got a gun?"

"Yeah, a shotgun. A Mossberg."

"Where does he stash it?"

She pointed to the dark space under the prep table. I yanked out my cell phone, turned it on and used it like a flashlight. Under the table, I spotted a shelf crowded with food cans.

"I don't see a gun. Would he ... would he lend it to the boys?"

"No, they got their own."

Great, wonderful.

Finally I caught a glint of steel. There behind the food tins was Jimmy's shotgun. I hauled it out.

"You know how to use it?" I asked.

She nodded. I handed it to her, though she could barely hold it.

She took a deep, shuddering breath. "When they find Jimmy, we're done for."

"Not if I can help it." I pulled out my gun. "You told me they wouldn't hurt you."

"I lied to make you leave." She leaned on the shotgun. "I don't know why I got mixed up in Jimmy's bad stuff. I used to be a good person."

"Maybe you still are."

A bang from the front of the diner sent my heart racing. I scrambled round the prep table over to the pass-through. Steeling myself, I stood up, pressed myself against the wall, and peered into the diner.

Another bang and another and another. The boys were trying to kick their way through the front door.

Suddenly, they quit. I strained to hear their voices, but between the throbbing car alarm and the rushing rain on the diner roof, I couldn't make out a thing.

"Where are they? What are they doing?" Gilda asked from the floor.

"I can't see them."

The minutes crawled by.

"Weird things went down here at night after Jimmy got mixed up with the boys," she said after a time. "At first, I figured my brain was going soft. Who'd want to believe that crazy stuff? But then … but then …" She let out a sob. "I got in too deep."

A huge blast thundered through the diner. The front door vanished. Nothing but splinters left round the frame. Wind and rain blew in through the opening.

Ears ringing, I forced myself to stay put by the pass-through.

"You're crazy, man!" Reilly shouted in his deep voice. "I told you. Jimmy's handling things. Gilda's with him. He took the old lady's keys, and now he's gonna kill *you* when he sees what you did. I'm outta here."

"Wait, bro. Go round back. See if his van's still there," Duane said.

"Gimme the shotgun. You can't be trusted."

"Then you give me your gun."

I risked a look. Duane was stepping through the ruined door into the diner. Wet streamed from his leather jacket and dripped onto the pistol in his fist — a Smith and Wesson by the looks of it. I steadied my gun.

"Jimmy! Reilly, get back here. *Reilly!*"

But Reilly didn't answer.

"They killed him!" Duane cried. "They killed him!"

I sighted through the pass-through opening and fired. Heard him cry out.

I hit the floor, expecting Duane to blast his way into the kitchen. Instead I heard the thud of steps on the porch, followed by swearing.

"Did you get him?" Gilda had clawed her way back up to her feet. Leaning against the prep table, she held the shotgun across her chest.

"Not sure. He took off."

The back windows over the kitchen grill looked out into woods beyond. I saw the top of Reilly's bald head pass by. Heard him splash through the mud at the back of the diner, not bothering to be quiet. After all, he had Duane's shotgun.

"Gilda, get away from the door." I crouched down beside the prep table. Readied my gun.

The back door flew open. Reilly burst in.

Gilda screamed.

The blast of his shotgun deafened me. Something stung my face like a horde of bees. A massive hole had appeared in the prep table, cutting it nearly in two. Fractured glass and crockery lay everywhere.

"Stop right there, Reilly!" Gilda held Jimmy's Mossburg steady, one hip against the ruins of the prep table.

"Gilda, are you crazy? Where's Jimmy?"

When she didn't answer, he swung the barrel in her direction. For the third time, an ear-shattering blast ripped through the diner.

Deaf from the noise, I saw that Gilda was still on her feet, but the kickback had wrenched the shotgun from her hands.

"Are you OK?" I managed to say. My voice sounded like it was underwater.

She slumped over the ruined prep table and stared at Reilly. He was a big guy, built like a bull, but the blast from Jimmy's Mossburg had blown him out the back door. One look and I could see he wasn't going to give us any more trouble.

"We have to get out of here," I said.

She couldn't hear me. I could barely hear myself. That's why we didn't see him until it was too late.

Duane crashed through the swing door into the kitchen. I caught a glint of light off a blade. Then he plunged Jimmy's hunting knife into Gilda's back.

I fired my Glock. Fired and kept firing until he fell.

Detritus crunched under my runners as I walked over to him. His face was as pale as his white-blond hair.

"Y-you shot me," he stammered, disbelief in his dying eyes.

"More than once," I said.

I went over to where Gilda had fallen. Her auburn hair had come loose. For a brief moment she looked young again.

"I left Jimmy's knife on the counter," she breathed. "I messed up."

She felt icy cold. I pulled out the BMW's key and turned off the car alarm.

In the welcome silence, she said, "I never meant to hurt you, Terry. I would never hurt a woman my age. Please say you believe me."

"I believe you." What did it hurt to lie?

"Terry …" Her voice was fading: I could barely hear her through the rain. "Look after this for me, will you?"

Her freezing fingers pressed Otto's lighter into my hand. I held her until she was gone, then slipped her precious talisman into my jeans.

I couldn't breathe. I had to get out of there. Gun in hand, I stumbled through the ruined front door into the cleansing rain. I let it wash the blood and violence from my face, my hands, my clothes ...

I was soaked through. The BMW started with no trouble. I turned out of the parking lot and headed back toward the interstate and civilization. By the time I reached that solitary closed gas station, the rain was tapering off.

Would I make Lexington by 5 a.m.? Not a chance.

I called Mike's cell. The relief I felt hearing his voice was pure joy.

"Mom! You OK? Where the hell are you?"

"I messed up. I ... I got lost."

"Listen to me. Don't go to the drop-off in Lexington. It's a trap."

"What?"

"There's a Dairy Queen on 9 2 2 half a mile before the Star-bucks. I'll pick you up there. Look for the black Mustang." He rang off.

Daylight was breaking. I drove south, my mind numb.

The way I figured it, Jimmy and his crew zoned in on cus-tomers travelling alone. Maybe Gilda got them talking, helped pick out the ones unlikely to be missed. Then Jimmy would take over while Duane and Reilly disappeared the cars through their chop shop. A nasty crime, but lucrative. Lots of swamp and wilderness around to hide the bodies. Little risk of getting caught if they didn't do it too often.

And how much of their bad business had Gilda been involved in? She certainly knew how to handle a shotgun. The more I thought about it, the less I wanted to know. I wanted to believe that she was a good person who'd been led down a dark rabbit hole by her passion to be extraordinary.

The Dairy Queen on 9 2 2 was easy to find; its sign shone like a beacon. A black Mustang was the only other car in the parking lot.

I called Mike again.

"I see you, Mom. Park next to me. Leave the keys in the BMW."

"Safe word?" I asked for the code word we'd use when he was a kid.

He laughed. "Godzilla."

I left the keys in the cup holder. I gathered up the maps, the burner phone, and the Glock and shoved them into the box he'd given me. My heart was churning as I grabbed the box and climbed into the safety of his car.

"Give me the burner," Mike said. I listened while he called and told someone where to find the BMW. When we turned back onto 9 2 2, I spotted a cluster of blue flashing lights coming toward us.

"You ratted on Reese and Marco," I said.

"I never wanted you involved, Mom. You don't know what I went through, those hours you were out of range."

I put it together. "You're a cop, aren't you? An undercover cop. Like your grandfather."

He stared through the windshield. "I couldn't tell you. You're safe now. Let's go home." He revved the motor, heading north back to Canada.

"You still got that gun?" he asked.

I nodded.

"Good," he said. "We'll deep-six it and the phone in a river on the way home. We'll forget this ever happened."

"Okay."

I felt for Otto's lighter in my jeans pocket. What would the American police make of the murder scene back at the diner? How deep would they dig? Would they simply write off the killings as a falling-out among thieves?

Whatever happened, I could never tell Mike about Mother's Diner. It would remain my darkest secret. Mine and Gilda's.

THE JACK WHYTE STORYTELLER'S AWARD

Tyner Gillies

Tyner, who also writes under the pen name Ty Caleb, is a full-time police officer and most-of-the-time writer from BC's Lower Mainland. He has released four novels with independent Canadian press Dark Dragon Publishing out of Toronto. He has an ongoing love affair with short fiction, has several stories published, and reads his own short fiction on his YouTube channel Ty Reads To You. Tyner's story 'Of Siege and Sword' appeared way back in Pulp Literature Issue 1, and 'The Lord of Lawn Ornaments' was seen more recently in Issue 24. He is repped by Stacey Kondla at The Rights Factory.

POLICE

◯When We Die

"Uh, Sarge?"

Sergeant James Kennedy looked up from the collision report he was reviewing to the young black-haired call-taker who stood in the door to his office. Her name was . . . Meena? Ameena? Amria? Getting old was a pain in the ass, and he couldn't remember shit.

"Yes, my young friend," he said, in lieu of her name. "What can I do for you?"

"Uh, there's a guy on the phone insisting on speaking to the watch commander."

James frowned. "Did he say what he wanted?"

She shook her head. "He was very polite. Says he has something important to discuss, but he won't talk to anyone but you. I mean, he didn't say *you* specifically, but he only wants to talk to the watch commander."

The plaque on the door to the office he shared with three other sergeants certainly said 'Watch Commander', so James figured he must be the man.

"Okay. Put him through, I guess."

She gave him a relieved smile and turned back to the small room that served as Daviston Detachment's radio room, where the single dispatcher and two call-takers worked. A handful of seconds later, the phone on his desk rang.

"Sergeant Kennedy, Daviston RCMP," he said when he picked up the receiver.

"Good evening, Sergeant," said a deep, not unpleasant voice on the other end of the line. "Is this the watch commander?"

"It is," James said. "What can I do for you?"

"And you're the highest rank in the city? The man in charge?"

James did not like where this was going. Generally, when someone was looking for 'the man in charge', they wanted to bust out a ridiculous conspiracy theory, like the Prime Minister was in league with Nazi terrorists and had sent a gang of raccoons to search their garbage for personal information.

James let out a long sigh. "Yes, that's me, I guess."

"Oh, excellent," the man said, sounding relieved. "I need some advice, and I didn't know where to turn. I figured the Mounties were the way to go."

"Right," James said, drawing the word out. "And what do you need advice on?"

"I'm trying to decide if I should end my life."

This James had not expected. He said nothing for several seconds.

"Are you still there, Sergeant?" the voice asked.

"Oh, er, yes, I am." His mind roiled, trying to think of something to say. "Uh, what did you say your name was?"

"My name is Brian."

James grabbed the A5 notebook beside his computer screen and picked up the pen that sat in the crease of the pages. "What's your last name, Brian?"

"I don't believe we've reached that point in our relationship, Sergeant. I'll be just Brian for now."

James half stood from his desk to see if he could wave down the call-taker. Now that he'd gotten over his initial shock and his brain had slipped back into gear, he needed to find out where this guy was so he could intervene. But she was back at her desk with her back to him, and she couldn't see his frantically waving arm.

"If you could just hang on a second, Brian, I need to—"

"No, Sergeant. If you leave or put me on hold, this conversation is over."

"All right," James said, and settled back into his chair. He was on his own. "How are you planning on killing yourself, Brian?"

"Oh, you misunderstand me, Sergeant. I won't be killing myself. I have an appointment for medical assistance in dying, and I'm trying to decide if I should keep it or not."

This, also, James had not expected. "Uh, okay. Why have you decided to do that?"

"I have cancer," Brian said.

"Oh," James said. He paused again, fishing around in the corners of his brain for what he should say next. "What kind of cancer do you have?"

"You know the kind that is easily treatable?"

"Sure."

"I have the other kind."

That was supremely unhelpful. "And is there any hope of getting better? Any treatment?"

"Oh, yes, there are treatment options. But they would only prolong my life for a short time. And that time would not be … pleasant."

James leaned forward and placed his elbows on his desk, the phone pressed to his ear. In nearly thirty years of uniform policing, he had talked to plenty of people who were suicidal, or at least pretending to be. And this guy was unlike any of them. There was no panic. No crisis. No miserable proclamations that the world would be better off without them. The man on the other end of the phone was calm, almost detached, and James found that far more unsettling than if he'd been railing and sobbing.

"Brian, why did you call here?"

The man on the other end of the line didn't say anything for a moment, but James could hear laboured breathing and knew he was still there.

After the space of five long breaths, Brian cleared his throat. "I … Well, I guess I'm scared, Sergeant."

"Call me James." It was very seldom that he ever encouraged 'clients' to call him by his first name, but this seemed like the time.

"All right, James," Brian said. "I'm scared and …" He paused for another long moment. "I want to know what you think happens to us when we die."

James sat back in his creaking office chair and ran a hand over his face. He was suddenly exhausted. Weary right down to his bones.

"I don't know if I'm the man you want to ask," James said.

"You don't believe in heaven?"

James sighed. He had a lot of opinions about spirituality and religion, but he was accustomed to keeping them to himself. But as he talked to this man who was reaching out to him for what was likely the hardest decision of his life, James didn't feel like now was the time for half-measures.

"I don't believe in God," James said, and he huffed out a long breath through his nose. "I have seen too many things in a lifetime of policing that refute the existence of a benevolent figure in the sky that is looking out for us. I am more inclined to agree with the Celts, or the old Norse. If there is a god, or maybe gods, they are fallible and human. Maybe a little mean-spirited.

"But I also think, if we live a good life and die well, we'll find peace in the end."

"I see," Brian said. He didn't sound surprised or disappointed, but James could hear the slightest waver in his voice. "And what if a man has not lived a good life?"

"I don't know," James said. "Do you have regrets?"

Brian let out a long, low chuckle. "The road of my life is paved with regrets, James. I can scarcely think, just now, of anything else."

All of James's instincts and training made him want to preserve this man's life, but he felt like he was running out of tarmac and couldn't get this intervention off the ground.

"Do you think, Brian," James said, "that there might be an opportunity to make amends for some of these regrets? Maybe earn yourself a little peace?"

Brian let out a long sigh that made a whooshing sound into the phone. "I have been ... trying. But my efforts have been fruitless. I don't think there is any more road in that direction."

"Is there any family you want to spend time with before, you know ..."

"Before I die?" Brian asked.

"Yeah. That."

Brian sighed again. "That is what I have been trying to do these last few days. But I'm afraid I have acted poorly in the past. Very poorly. And the children I ignored most of their lives are now ignoring me." He let out another long breath. "And rightfully so, I suppose."

There was a small hitch in Brian's voice, the first since this conversation began, and James felt his heart give a bit of a lurch as he heard it.

"And there is no one you want to spend time with? A friend? A colleague? Anyone?"

"No," Brian said, his voice cracking in earnest now. "There is no one."

For a moment James could hear nothing but his own heartbeat crashing in his ears, as he thought frantically of something to say to this man, who had reached out to him for … What? For guidance? For help? Hope?

"Is there anything you've always wanted to do, Brian? I mean anything? Jump out of an airplane? Go on an African safari? Go on a date with a high-end escort? Anything?"

Brian chuckled softly. "Believe it or not, Sergeant, I've done all of those things. I have lived my life for myself. I worked hard, played even harder, and did exactly as I pleased. And that is why I find myself alone. Alone at the end."

"I wish there was something I could tell you that would make you feel better," James said, and meant it.

"Me as well, Sergeant," Brian said. He cleared his throat and let out what sounded almost like a growl. "That brings me back to my original question. Do you think I should keep my appointment at the clinic tomorrow? Should I end my life?"

"Where are you right now?"

Brian sighed, a little exasperation creeping into the sound. "I am nowhere near you right now, and you won't be able to find me. I'll be travelling early tomorrow. Now, please, help me. Do you think I should end my life?"

James found himself shaking his head in the quiet of his

office. "That is a terrible thing for you to ask of me. You know that, don't you?"

"It is. And I'm sorry. But I'm asking anyway."

James took a long, steadying breath, as much to buy himself time as to get oxygen. "I want you to promise me, fucking promise me, that you will think very carefully if there is anything you need to do in life before the end. And that if you come up with something, you'll pursue it." He took another breath. "Will you do that for me?"

There was a long pause. "Yes, James. I will do that for you. I promise."

"Good."

"And if I don't come up with anything?"

James took another long breath, and didn't feel at all steady by it. "Then keep your appointment."

"Thank you, James."

James wanted to say more. But his tank was empty. He didn't feel like he could remember his own name, let alone say anything meaningful to the man on the other end of the phone. Finally, he said, "I'm going to be at this desk all night. If you need to talk, or vent, or curse, I want you to call me. Will you do that?"

"I will," Brian said. "Thank you, James. I'm glad I called you."

James was about to say he was welcome, but the line went dead and Brian was gone.

He got up from his desk and went into the radio room. The young black-haired call-taker spun in her chair when he came in.

"How did that go, Sarge?"

James rubbed his stubbly chin, thinking about how much to reveal, and decided as little as possible was for the best. "Can you tell me where that call originated?"

She turned back to her desk, grabbed her mouse, and clicked several boxes on the CAD — computer-aided dispatch — screen. "The call came from an internet-based phone number."

She pointed to the box she'd brought up, and James leaned close to the screen. The originating call number was just a meaningless series of numbers and letters.

"So there's no way to trace it," James said.

"I'm sorry, no."

"Okay. Thanks." He turned back to his office.

"Is there anything for us to worry about?"

He stopped and looked over his shoulder at her. "Nothing for you to worry about at all." He would do enough worrying for the both of them.

For the rest of the night, every time his desk phone rang, James scrabbled for it, hoping it would be Brian. It never was, though. And by the end of the night he was so tired he felt like he'd spent the whole shift fighting rather than sitting at a desk.

When he was relieved at o 6 o o hours, he sat in front of his locker, his uniform half-off, for a long time, staring at the piece of floor between his scuffed boots. He could not believe that a man would end his life and there was nothing he could do about it. He had been a cop his entire adult life, and for the first time, he felt like he had failed in his duty.

This could not be the way this ended.

With a purpose in mind, he changed quickly and walked out to his truck. Once he'd fired up the engine and his phone was connected to Bluetooth, he called his wife.

"Hello, lovey," she said. He could hear the bathroom tap running as she put on her makeup for her work day.

"Good morning, beautiful."

"What's up? You on your way home?"

"Not just yet. There's something I have to do." As briefly as he could, he told her about the conversation he'd had with Brian.

"Oh my God," his wife said. "What are you going to do?"

"I don't know yet. But I have to do *something*."

"Okay, babe. Whatever you do, just be careful, okay?"

"I will. I promise."

The regional hospital that housed the MAID clinic was about forty-five minutes outside of Daviston, and James pulled his truck onto the highway and pressed the pedal down. The big engine roared as he navigated the winding road. He desperately wanted some caffeine but didn't believe he could spare the time.

Thirty-seven minutes later, at ten minutes after seven, James pulled into the hospital parking lot. He had no idea if this hospital was Brian's destination, but he assumed the man had some kind of ties to the area if he'd called Daviston detachment. He stepped into the lobby, which was still and quiet at this time of the morning, and found a seat facing the door.

All of this was a gamble, and he had no idea if it was going to pay off or not.

The foot traffic into the building picked up after seven-thirty, and every time the entrance doors *shooshed* open, James sat up straighter and craned his neck to see who was coming inside. Then, at nine minutes before eight, James thought his gamble might have paid off.

The doors made that *shooshing* sound, and James saw a man, a decade or so older than he was, dressed in khaki slacks and a light jacket, walk slowly into the lobby. He had a short, neatly kept beard, more grey than brown, and his head was buzzed down to stubble. The man had his eyes on the floor in front of him, and his hand was pressed to his side as though he had an ache there.

James got out of his seat and approached him.

The man looked up, then stopped. His blue eyes narrowed, and then a slight grin curved one corner of his mouth.

"Hello, James," the blue-eyed man said.

"Hello, Brian."

"You can't stop me," Brian said. "I'm not doing anything illegal. And I'm in my right mind."

James had thought hard, almost painfully hard, as he'd made the drive here. And up until that moment he had no idea what he was going to say. But, suddenly, he knew.

"I'm not here to stop you." He stepped forward and slid his arm under the hand that wasn't pressed to Brian's side, gently lifting the man's arm so it draped over James' shoulders. Brian smelled subtly of Irish Spring soap.

"I'm here so you don't have to make this walk alone."

The older man tightened his arm around James' shoulders and lowered his head. Then he sniffed loudly and took a step forward, James stepping with him.

"Thank you, my friend," he said. "I'm very glad you're here."

James hooked his arm around the other man's waist, and together they followed the signs for the MAID clinic.

THE BUMBLEBEE FLASH FICTION CONTEST

THE 2025 BUMBLEBEE FLASH FICTION CONTEST

It has been another sweet year for the hive, and we at *Pulp Literature* would like to thank each bumblebee out there for their contributions to our shortest flash fiction contest. A special thanks goes to our endlessly talented beekeeper (judge), Bob Thurber, who thoroughly enjoyed this year's batch of stories and extends his congratulations to all of the shortlisted authors.

As always, your stingers were sharp but your stories were sharper, and we were bee-yond impressed at this year's buzz-worthy and un-bee-lievable talent.

Now, enough bee puns—let's bee-hold our Queen Bee and our winners!

Winner:
Cadence Mandybura with 'Coin Girl'

Unranked Honourable Mentions:
Katherine Weeks with 'Bonfire Night'
Rosanna Elves with 'The Last Twenty-Four Hours'

Ultimately, the winning story won over Bob as "an eerie and concise tale packed with peculiarities." He also offered "acknowledgements" and "approving nods" to these two honourable mentions alongside his congratulations to all the shortlisted authors.

The 2025 shortlist, in alphabetical order:

Shauna Grace Andrews with 'No Soap'
Boston Hall with 'Urticaria'
Boston Hall with 'You Heard Naught but Your Blood'
Sandra Kasturi with 'Beard of Birds'
Cadence Mandybura with 'After Mina's Prayer Gets Answered'
Nick Stacey with 'Statuesque'
Brooke A Yates with '12.95'

Cadence Mandybura's award-winning speculative fiction has appeared in Metaphorosis, Tales & Feathers, and Orca, as well as in Pulp Literature issues 29, 35, and 37. Cadence is a graduate of the Writer's Studio at Simon Fraser University and a past associate producer for the fiction anthology podcast The Truth. She likes to drum. Find her at CadenceMandybura.com.

Katherine Weeks is thirty-seven and has been working on one full-length novel or another since she was fifteen. She has published seven books on Amazon Kindle.

Rosanna Elves is a Canadian-Mexican author living in the picturesque city of Victoria, BC. A mother, identical twin, and globetrotter, Rosanna has lived in Japan, Peru, and Mexico: experiences that infuse her fiction, poetry, and children's books. Her writing has been found in The New Canadian Stories, Stripes Literary Magazine, Black Hare Press, and parABnormal Magazine. She has also earned a Rising Star Award in the Sunshine Coast Writers and Editors Society's Beachcombers 50th Anniversary Anthology (2022). Rosanna is working on her second children's book, which is forthcoming this year.

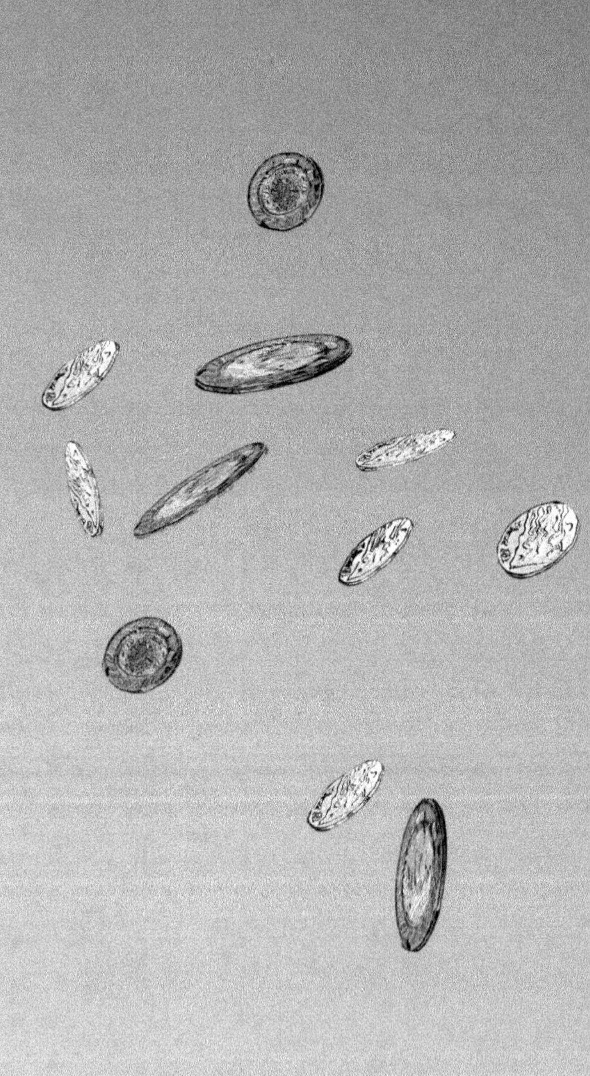

Coin Girl

BY CADENCE MANDYBURA

Adora rubs her forearm, where the bud of a coin itches against her bone. Catching the gleam of her older sister watching from the other side of the coach, Adora turns the gesture to a scratch and swat, as though pestered by a fly. Liya nudges her chin forward, and fear floods Adora.

Liya knows.

Adora leans back into her nest and pretends to go to sleep like her younger siblings, slumping against the long hours of travel. She can talk to Liya at the next town, after the obligatory performance. She thinks, dreads, that she needs Liya's help. But who else can she trust?

The coins are getting stuck. And without the coins, Adora is nothing.

The crowd is sparse and squinty in the midday heat, not much charmed by Bess and Boster's clown routine. The young ones are the warm-up act, attracting an audience while Adora waits backstage, sweating in her puffed dress. Her mother tuts and yanks the hem closer to Adora's ankles.

"Another growth spurt," mutters Mother. Father dabs makeup on a pimple above Adora's left eye. Her parents' irritation grinds in the hot shade like sandpaper. Liya's already out in the audience.

A few slaps of applause as Bess and Boster take their bows. Adora walks out with her mandolin, giving the little ones a bright smile and chucking them under the chin. They grin back, and no one can tell how much they all hate each other.

Once, it was only Adora's extraordinary musical talent that divided them. Then came the coins, and her parents' favour poisoned any affection between the siblings. They still resent Adora getting extra helpings of food, even though she now tries to share it back.

Adora starts with a pretty étude. The coin in her arm is a blunt annoyance as she picks through arpeggios, hoping the applause will help coax the metal to the surface.

During a virtuosic flourish, she hits a sour note when she meets Liya's suspicious stare. Liya isn't part of the show; she's never been cute enough for the stage. Her job is to drum up tips and manage their finances.

Adora skims her gaze away and carries on playing, her face prickly. The pennies they get from performances aren't enough. If this coin doesn't come soon, there won't be any food to go around, no matter how carefully Liya plans.

After the show, the children have a few hours to rest as their parents pump the town for anyone interested in a salon recital. Bess and Boster run off to explore, leaving Adora and Liya to fold up their stage and assemble dinner.

Adora waffles on how to ask Liya for help, but she doesn't need to. As soon as they're in the stuffy privacy of the coach, Liya grabs Adora's arm, palpating until she finds the lump. Adora squirms but knows better than to cry out.

"It's stuck?" says Liya.

"I don't know."

Liya shakes her head, rejecting Adora's indecision. "We should cut it out."

"What? No." Adora wants to yank her arm back, but Liya's hands are firm.

"It's probably your last coin. Don't you see what's happening?"

Adora's pimple throbs. "But it's in my arm. I might not be able to play again …"

Liya takes Adora's hands, a surge of warmth. "Dory. This could be a good thing. We could …"

But Adora shrinks, and the earnestness in Liya's gaze hardens. She drops Adora's hands and flicks the lace ruff at Adora's shoulder. "Get out of this stupid thing and help me with dinner."

There is no recital that night.

Pain rips Adora from sleep. She is pinned — her mouth is blocked — the sharp line across her forearm muddles to a hungry, seeking press of fingers that won't stop, won't stop, *just won't stop*

and Adora is flailing, screaming, she hits hot breath and hair, a shoulder, but it's not enough

a metallic wrench and the weight on her is gone

and everyone is shouting, Adora is shaking and wet, her hand over the warm syrupy spill of her arm.

Later, when she's bandaged and the world comes back into aching focus, they find the knife Liya used to cut open her sister. The coin, and Liya, are gone.

No one knows what to say. Bess and Boster look at the floor, her parents up to God. But Adora has nothing, is nothing, coinless, too empty even for tears.

Six awards for genre-busting fiction and poetry

The Bumblebee Flash Fiction Contest
Deadline: 15 February
Prize: $300

The Magpie Award for Poetry
Deadline: 15 April
First Prize: $500

The Hummingbird Flash Fiction Prize
Deadline: 15 June
Prize: $300

The First Page Cage
Deadline: 30 September
Prize: $300

The Raven Short Story Contest
Deadline: 15 October
Prize: $300

The Kingfisher Poetry Prize
Deadline: 15 October
Prize: $300

pulpliterature.com/contests

$\mathcal{B}$ONFIRE NIGHT

BY KATHERINE WEEKS

I only remember bits and pieces of that Bonfire Night when I was seven. We parked at the top of a multi-storey car park with fluorescent lights in the ceiling and shadows in the corners. We walked through the big field, past fairground rides covered with gurning cartoon characters. We bought toffee apples and stood by the fire. It was the first time I'd actually seen them burn a Guy.

I mean, I know what I've been *told*. Should have known. Seedy place. Seedy people. We should have turned round and left. Not safe. But that's not what I remember.

I remember the jewellery being sold in the stalls, all mesmerizing in deep reds and blues. *Cheap plastic,* my parents say when I mention it, *Real jewels aren't as gaudy as that.* I remember the crowds of people, and how everyone went silent in wonder when the fireworks went off. *No crowd control—lax safety standards.* I remember the group of kids my age, two boys and a girl, who asked me if I wanted to come and see their tree-house. They'd built it themselves, they said.

Luring her in, my parents told each other later. *Probably sent over by some creep waiting in the shadows.* But I never saw any creep. Just those three kids and the little pile they'd made in the gap between the roots of two trees that had grown together. It wasn't what I'd pictured when they'd said 'tree-house', but I was impressed all the same. A mound of wooden boxes, rabbit hutches mostly, with tunnels knocked through them so we could crawl around and sit in them.

Think about it — where do you think they got those rabbit hutches from? If they didn't steal them, then someone else did. Think about what kind of people they were.

I don't remember their names. I don't remember what we talked about, though I know we *did* talk. I think we spent most of our time marvelling at the night, watching the fireworks go off from deep within our secret hiding place.

Death trap. You could have been badly hurt. But I wasn't the one who got hurt — it was one of the boys. He crawled through a tunnel and jarred one of the walls by mistake, and a ton of splintered wood collapsed on his head.

I was the one closest to the exit. I told them I'd go and get help.

I don't want to talk about it. I don't want to think about it. What could have happened.

It seemed to take hours to find my parents.

Leave it alone. Can't you see that this is hurting me?

When I did find them, they didn't seem to hear a word I said. They told me how long they'd been looking for me. How they'd heard I'd gone off with strangers. How we were leaving, right now, no arguments.

Well, there's nothing we can do about it now. So why dredge up bad memories?

I was crying and protesting all the way back to the car park. They didn't look back once.

I thought you were the kind of girl who knew how to rise above the drama.

I never saw those three other children again. I never found out what happened next. Whether they managed to get help in time, or whether they sat there, waiting for me, until it was too late.

Should have known. Seedy place. Seedy people. We should have turned round and left. Not safe.

The Last Twenty-Four Hours

by Rosanna Elves

Remote, you said. Quiet and idyllic, you said. I'll be focused. That's what *you* said.

I only ever wanted peaceful solitude. Somehow, you convinced me that your family's hideout, buried in the wild woods, would be the perfect writing retreat.

The wastebasket cowers in the corner, hidden by my crumpled words.

The wind mocks me. Its solemn howls were a soothing background to the clacking keys of my typewriter for the *first* hour. Now they tear at the cabin's weathered siding, knowing I cannot escape.

No distractions, you said. You said fifty hours out of the month is worth it. You don't care one way or the other if I enter this contest. What were your real motivations for bringing me here? How did I *ever* let you convince me to hand over my phone?

You left me here.

Enough rations for two days, you said. You didn't account for my anxious pillaging to satiate nerves. How do you *not* know this about me? Empty plastic and tin carcasses strewn across the small space remind me of my gluttonous infractions. I'll never make it the forty-eight hours until you retrieve me. I'll starve to death wrapped in this bearskin rug, also abandoned in front of this useless fireplace.

A wood-burning fire is stimulating to the senses, you said. You know I've never lit a fire in my life, *ever*. It's easy, you said. After a dozen unstimulating attempts to ignite something other than newsprint, I am resolved to let anger wrap its heat around me.

With knocking knees and bearskin shoulders, I sit at the table in one last attempt of the day to write a semblance of a story. I think I'll write about a mythical creature and its familiar tropes. You would *hate* it.

Dusk has begun to descend.

The rickety lantern, as old as the cabin, sets the contrast on my blank page. The light and dark begin to blur together. I am drawn to movement at the window. There's nothing to fear in these woods, you said. You *know* I don't like the dark.

The gas lantern lets out a high-pitched whistle and the light sizzles out. I sit there, thinking about you, with narrowed eyes. My ears adjust first and, between the howls, I hear footsteps.

I *refuse* to be the female in *that* cliché. Shrugging off the bearskin, I feel my way to the hunting rifle hung above the mantel and cock the empty chamber. I stand my ground.

"I'm ready," I say.

SICH PAY

Helena Pantsis

Helena Pantsis (she/they) *is an editor, writer, and artist from Naarm, Australia, with a fond appreciation for the weird, the dark, and the experimental. She is the author of short story collection* GLUTT, *and the forthcoming poetry collection* Captcha. *More can be found at hlnpnts.com.*

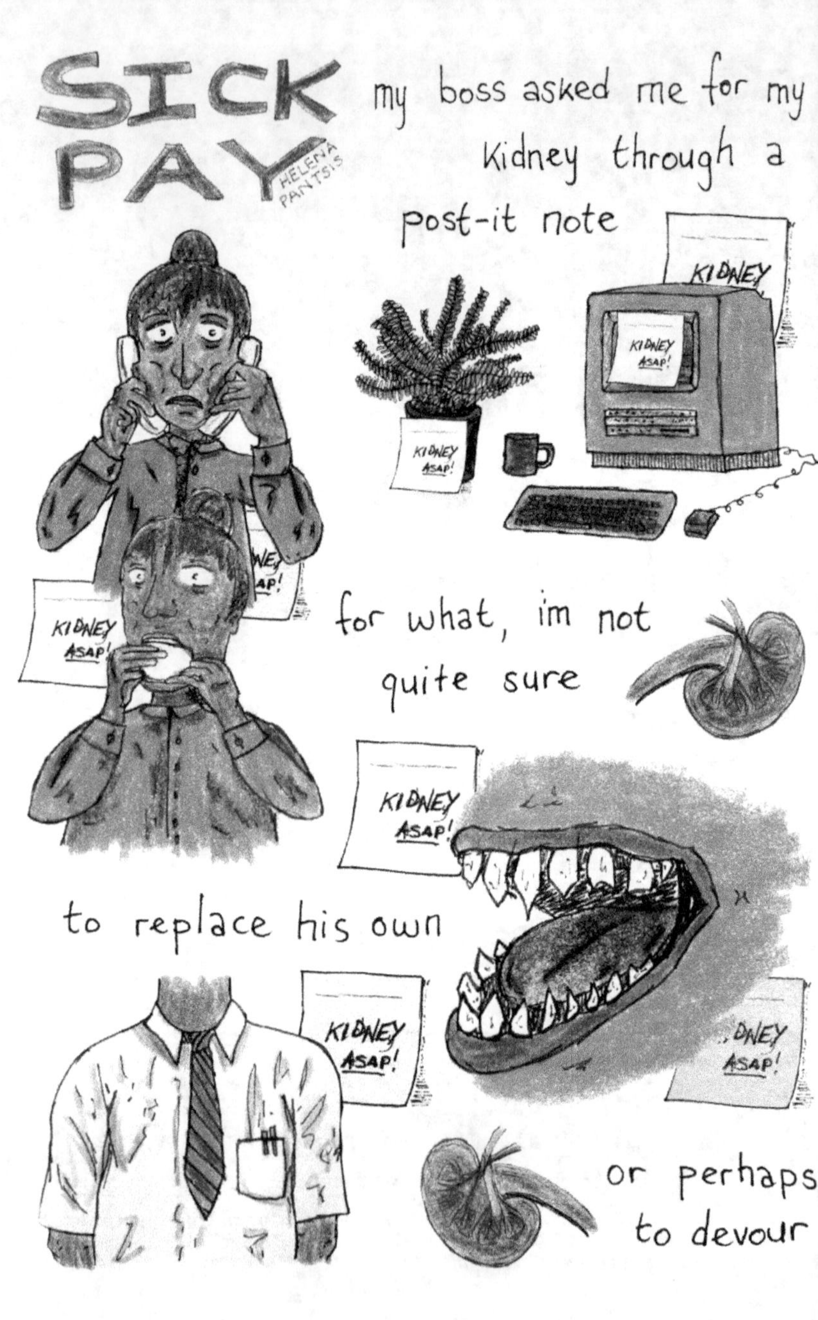

SICK PAY
HELENA PANTSIS
my boss asked me for my kidney through a post-it note
KIDNEY
KIDNEY ASAP!
KIDNEY ASAP!
KIDNEY ASAP!
for what, im not quite sure
KIDNEY ASAP!
to replace his own
KIDNEY ASAP!
...DNEY ASAP!
or perhaps to devour

or simply to remind
me that he can.

KIDNEY ASAP!
KIDNEY ASAP!
KIDNEY ASAP!

it's written
in the contract i signed

to give
the body
over
entirely

KIDNEY ASAP!

despite its
misgivings
& the things
it already lacks

KIDNEY ASAP!
KIDNEY ASAP!

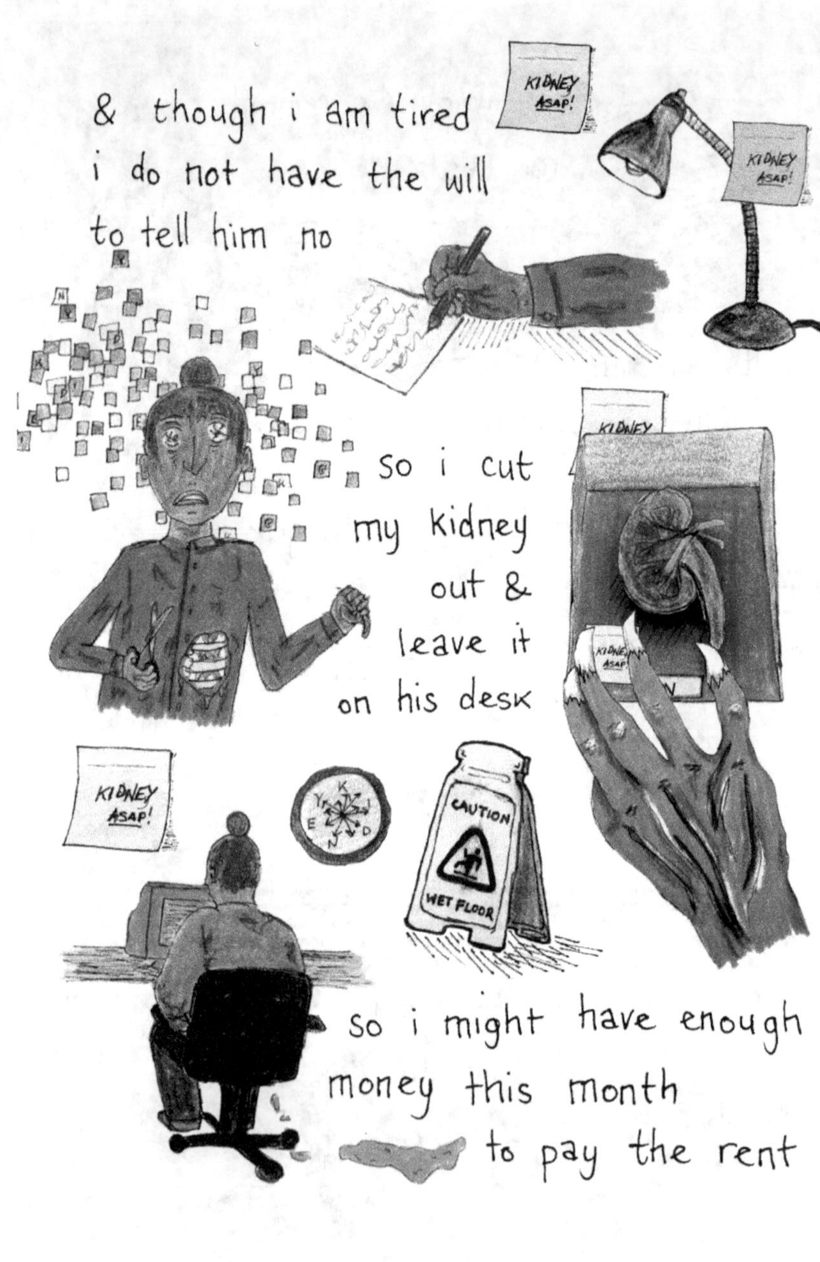
& though i am tired
i do not have the will
to tell him no

so i cut
my kidney
out &
leave it
on his desk

so i might have enough
money this month
to pay the rent

KIDNEY ASAP!
KIDNEY ASAP!
KIDNEY
KIDNEY ASAP!
KIDNEY ASAP!
CAUTION
WET FLOOR

LET ME TELL YOU A STORY

Mel Anastasiou

Mel Anastasiou writes the Fairmount Manor Mysteries, the Hertfordshire Pub Mysteries, and the Monument Studios Mysteries. Winner of a Literary Titan Gold award and shortlisted for the Leacock Medal, Mel is also the author of two illustrated thirty-day workbooks on story structure: the steampunk-themed The Writer's Boon Companion and The Writer's Friend and Confidante. We're delighted to present this story, which forms the first part of her novel Younger Men, due out from Pulp Literature Press in 2026. For news on published and upcoming works, visit Mel's website, melanastasiou.wordpress.com.

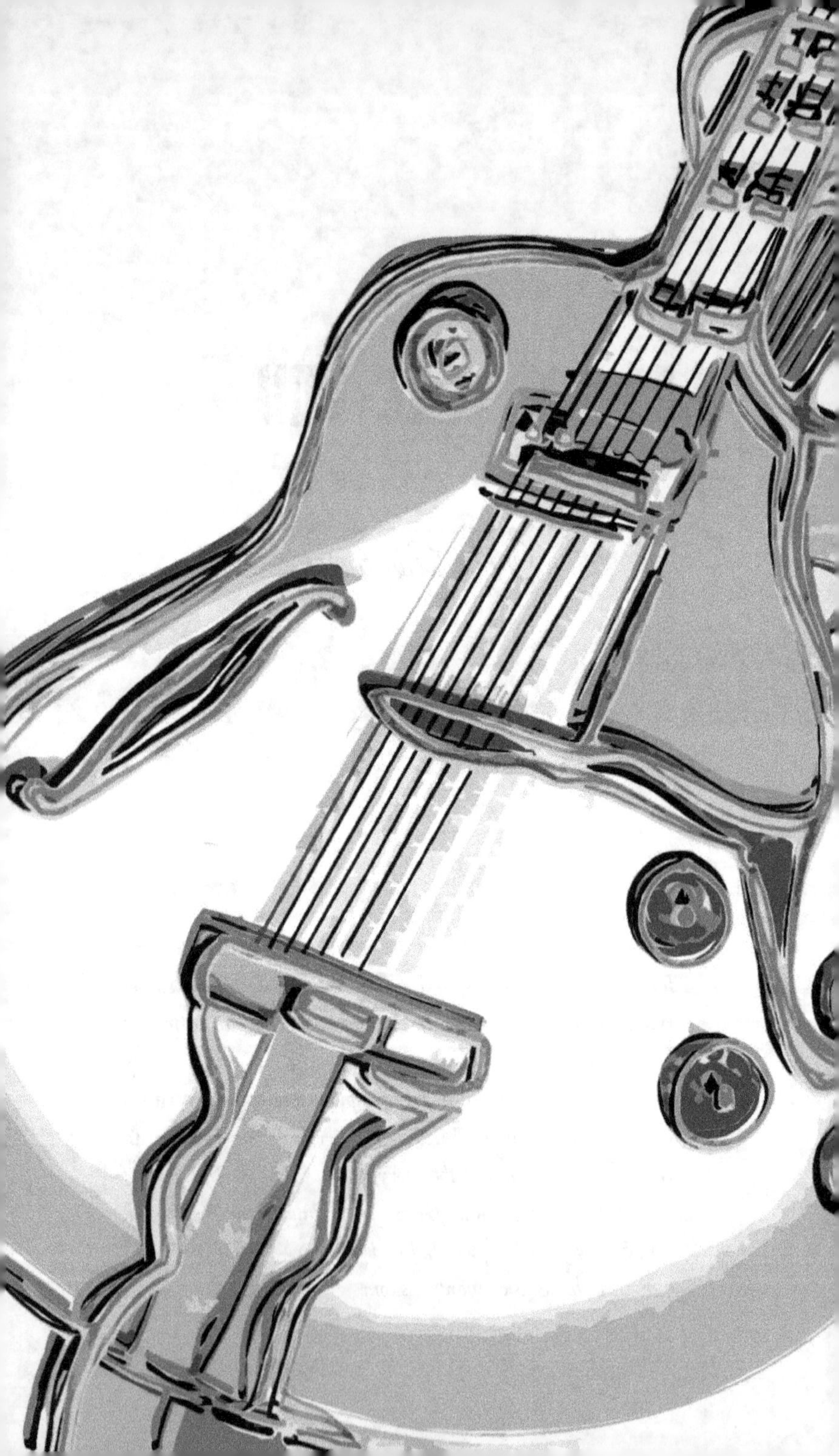

*L*et Me Tell You a Story

The second Friday in September, Louisa made the whole staff of Westside Elementary School go on the Zombie Walk. Regardless of age or degree of fitness, regardless of skin sensitivity to makeup or religious objections to the occult, we all had to bloody our faces, rip our clothes, and go. When we looked dubious, she scowled around the staff room table. "You cowards, shape up. This is something you need to do for Hayley's sake."

"You're all so kind," I said. "But for the one hundredth time, Louisa, there's nothing wrong with me."

Considering Louisa's small stature, unpopularity, and extreme good looks, I would like to think that all my teaching colleagues sat up and voted yes was due to the power of her crusading spirit. But later, when we were chopping our salads in the staff room kitchen, Apollo wondered aloud to Louisa whether it was entirely a good idea to use the undead to try to cheer up the recently divorced. He pointed at me. "Case in point, Hayley has cut her finger again." Louisa slapped the knife out of my hand and chopped my arugula for me.

So, that Friday afternoon, we Westside Elementary staff left our classrooms to totter in ragged clothing, past office buildings and bus stops and parked cars, and join the Zombie Walk in shiny-glass downtown Vancouver, our pockets stuffed with tubes of fake blood. Louisa brought a bullhorn, and no sooner had she merged us with hundreds of other zombies than she took the whole thing over.

"What do you want?" Louisa bullhorned at us zombies.

"*Blood,*" we shouted back. I met Apollo's eye under his baseball cap, and he gave me a guilty look. I knew why, too. Somehow being in a crowd of zombies made you actually want blood. I smeared a picture window with red paint. A woman at a computer on the other side shrank back. She could probably feel the bloodlust.

"I can't hear you," Louisa bellowed at the mob. "What do you want?"

"*Blood.*"

"When do you want it?"

"*Urghurerearrr.*" The wordless cry.

Tip your head to the side — right or left, just pick one and stick with it. Roll your eyes, hands out, and totter back and forth. That's how you do the Zombie Walk. It's simple enough, and simple pleasures can amuse, at least for a while. Then we saw the tourist bus.

"*Bus . . . bus,*" we cried, and moved as one zombie towards the blue double-decker. If I hadn't been a zombie I might have felt sorry for those pale hands and faces pressed against the windows — especially the poor devils on the top deck. But the

Zombie Walk is part of Vancouver's touristic charm. (To appreciate it best, you might rather zombie than be zombied.)

Hands outstretched, moaning, we staggered up to the bus and smeared it with red. As a kindergarten teacher, I like to keep an open, uncritical attitude, but someone unclear on the concept of national identities seemed to be in charge of stencilling Union Jacks on Vancouver tourist buses. It seemed like a bizarre and unnecessary kind of national cross-dressing to me, but even so I wiped the blood off the flag of the mother country with my sleeve. It felt a bit like poster paint and a bit like something you'd find in a Kleenex.

At a kick in the head, I looked up to see Louisa poised atop Apollo's shoulders, smearing as high as she could reach, which was not very high. The bus passengers had their cameras out to snap photos left and right. They appeared to be experiencing a common sense of armoured safety within the bus walls, right up to the moment someone forced the back door of the bus — or else a good sport inside opened the door — and a horde of the undead flocked inside. Those of us still outside were practically rocking the bus, and there seemed to be a bit of a traffic jam around us.

I said to my principal Julia, as she smeared beside me, "This is bonding for us as a staff."

"I hope so." Julia fingerpainted two concentric circles of fake blood on the bus. Somehow Julia made being undead appear both graceful and inevitable. "We're all glad you're enjoying yourself."

"I do wish you all would stop worrying. Especially when half the staff is divorced themselves, and they know I'll get through it."

Julia raised an eyebrow. "I'm glad you said that. Have you considered that your restlessness might mean that you've outgrown your job?"

"I love teaching kindergarten."

"Yet everyone's afraid you're thinking of transferring away from Westside. I think you need to look at your professional development."

"Sure. Maybe." I was smearing madly now. I backed into the middle of the road to admire our handiwork, and that was when the car hit me.

Now, there were a lot of zombies around that day, so I'll give that driver credit for hitting only one out of hundreds of us. As well, the imitation chaos and fear that are vital to Zombie Walks might confuse a driver, especially if, as was the case with the car that hit me, his windshield was smeared with fake blood. So I would like to give that driver the benefit of the doubt — and myself, as well, for no matter what Louisa or anybody else might say about it, I did not step in front of that car on purpose.

The car hit me side-on. I had time to think my last thoughts and time to appreciate that I had time to think my last thoughts, as the Vitara caught me on the leg with a bruising blow, knocked over a concrete pot of bright green laurel — you see how danger heightens the senses — and skinned an iron spirit bear before careening back into the traffic.

Julia caught me. She and a few of the other worried undead dragged me off the road towards the bus. "How badly are you hurt?"

"I'm all right." My chest felt tight, but my eyes were dry.

"Oh, Hayley, I'm so sorry. Here I'm proposing to mentor you, and I couldn't even keep you safe from traffic."

Louisa kicked her way down off Apollo's shoulders and shoved through the crowd. "I'm a doctor. Let me through." Louisa didn't even have her St John's.

The zombies rumbled tighter around me.

"Don't move her."

"She's standing up." Scattered applause rippled through the crowd.

"Oh, my God, she's got blood on her," somebody gasped.

"We've all got blood on us," somebody else said. "We're *zombies*."

Apollo bent over me. "Are you hurt?"

I looked up at my friends. "I'm a little hurt, but I'll live."

"Let me see your hip," Julia said. "Apollo, you have your St Johns—what do you think?"

Louisa said, "Oh, everybody thinks they're a doctor. Medical school is no picnic, you know." She bent down to hiss in my ear. "I see what you're trying to do, Hayley, and I'm not having it."

"It was an accident. I didn't see the car."

"That had better be true. And don't you dare leave Westside. I'm surrounded by fools with teaching degrees. I need you, so stop being so damned unhappy and restless."

"I'm not."

"Shh! I'll find a way to fix you."

"I'm *fine*." I held on to my hip.

"She doesn't need fixing, she needs a change," Apollo said. "Hayley, after twenty years in one place, maybe it's time for something new. To be different. Like that guy over there."

It was true. In the shadow of the blood-smeared tour bus stood one who was different. He wasn't wearing ragged pyjamas or a torn T-shirt and shorts. His face was not covered in blood. He wasn't, indeed, one of us. The man stepped forward, patting the media equipment slung around his body. He rubbed one green Croc against the back of his khakis and identified himself. "CLKC Radio Vancouver."

Louisa said, "Stand back. Let this radio guy get over here and interview Hayley. *She* was almost killed."

The radio guy slipped towards me through the crowd.

Louisa raised her bullhorn and bellowed, "Come on, all you zombies. Finish off the tour bus. You wanna live forever?"

They tottered after her, leaving me face to face with the radio man and his microphone. I feared microphones, although it was not a sexual thing.

He sat down close beside me. "Hayley, just now you were almost killed. The nation wants to know: what is a zombie's last thought before death?"

"I didn't actually —"

He pushed the mic closer. "As a zombie, was this last thought the same as your last thought before your *previous* death?"

A funny man. I supposed that radio was bound to send a funny man to a Zombie Walk. It made perfect directorial sense, but I couldn't tell a funny radio man my real last thoughts. Last thoughts are pretty damned personal, whether trivial or life-changing. But I couldn't tell a waiting nation of listeners to go to hell either, so I simply answered, "*Urghurerearrr.*"

He laughed and strode away without a backward look, his green Crocs flashing in the sun. Apollo, Julia, and I were on our own, with the crowd of zombies gone and only the tourists still trapped in the bus looking down upon us. With the arm not holding me upright, Apollo scratched his head under his baseball cap. Fake blood did itch.

Louisa tore back to us, leaving her ragtag band of zombies leaderless. "What did you tell him were your last thoughts? They'd better be good."

"Something about the rewards of a life spent helping children?" Julia stroked my hair back from my brow. "Arguably the best thing about teaching is that you never waste a day of your life."

Louisa said, "Hayley, if you're so pathetic that your last thoughts are about teaching, that must mean you're staying at Westside."

Julia said, "Hayley's going to become a vice-principal."

"No, she's not," Louisa snapped. "The board transfers vice-principals to other schools. They transfer them on a dime."

"For the greater good," Julia replied.

"For their evil plots," Louisa said.

Apollo interrupted. "*I* know Hayley's last thoughts."

"No, you don't," Louisa said. "What are they?"

"I'm not telling Hayley's innermost secrets. Are you really not hurt, Hayley?"

"I wish everybody would listen to me," I complained. "I'm hurt but not too hurt."

Julia said, "They would listen to you if you became a vice-principal."

Louisa said, "We don't believe Hayley wants that."

Apollo said, "What exactly is it that you want, Hayley?"

The question surprised and terrified me. "You mean forever?"

"He means now," Julia said. "We all mean now."

We gazed into the seething mob. I remembered my last thoughts and wondered, what if the car had killed me? What would I wish for if I were properly dead and couldn't have it?

I didn't know. But Louisa, Apollo, and Julia were waiting, and I had to say something.

So I said, "I would like a well-poured Guinness."

Even with the best-poured Guinness in the Lower Mainland on the table before me, it was sad to be undead and alone in the middle of the teachers' pub.

Somehow, I'd missed that Friday afternoon moment when all the teachers move on towards the weekend. The younger teachers leave for dates, the older ones pick up pizza for the kids. So there among the civilians I sat, still dressed like a zombie, alone at a table for twelve on a Friday night. I felt like the last zombie in the world.

At a touch on my shoulder, I turned to see the waiter with a tray in his hand, gazing down at my Guinness. There was an inch of the dark liquid left in my glass. Something floated on the surface — cheese, possibly.

"Sorry," he said. "You going to finish that?"

"No, take it," I told him. "Thanks."

The waiter was a young fellow, a good-looking boy with long hair tied back and a slim build under a white shirt. The kind of boy I'd have been attracted to when I was as young as he. The years leading to my present age seemed to plunge behind me like the sides of a vast canyon.

The waiter took a wet terry cloth and wiped the table, missing the sticky bits, stacking glasses on his tray. There was a jumble of bills we teachers had left as tips, and he pocketed those. He pointed to a pack of cigarettes one of Apollo's buddies had left on the table. "Those your cigarettes?"

"No," I told him, but I put the smokes in my bag to give to Apollo. The pack felt warm in my hand, and for a moment I almost wished that I hadn't quit smoking twenty years before. I remembered moments when pulling out a cigarette, lighting it, and taking that first deep drag made me feel — inaccurately of course — both sensuous and self-confident.

The waiter snatched glances at me as he worked. What did he see? Some lady in a zombie get-up, I guessed. Someone who looked like his mother, or like the mother of one of his friends. A couple next to me kissed and fed each other chips. They appeared about to burst with smooth-skinned sexuality.

"Are you okay?" the waiter asked.

"Sorry, do I look ill? It's the make-up."

"More the fake blood. But you look sad, even for a zombie."

"I believe" — I counted on my fingers — "that you're the thirtieth kind person this week to ask me whether I'm all right."

"If it makes a difference, I can tell you that even dressed as a zombie you are easy on the eyes. In fact, you may be the loveliest zombie in the world."

There's probably nothing nicer than that to say to the sorrowful undead. I thanked him.

He said, "Are you dealing with heartbreak or something?"

"A little bit. Divorced, that sort of thing." I felt restless, and fed up with feeling special after the divorce, like a reverse bride. "But everybody's kind of broken, aren't they?"

He cleared his throat, set his tray on the table, and sat down. "You know, I always figured broken was in some ways a good thing. Like, who wants to be a tile when you could be a mosaic?"

I blinked. "Your theory merits careful consideration."

The waiter said, "I'm Charles."

The couple at the next table were now necking openly across the chip bag.

I stood. "I'm Hayley."

He held out his hand. I shook it. I caught a bus towards home, and, dressed as I was, the other passengers left me alone while I tried to decide whether I felt like a mosaic. Which was to say, a little on the ancient side but with educational properties, and retaining much of my original grout around the edges.

CHAPTER 2

When you've been married as long as I was, and then you stop, it's like you're the captain of a submarine coming back to land after twenty years of service in the dark depths. You stumble around, a blinking innocent, your hairstyle slightly out of date and your ears popping under the pressure of being single for the first time since you trod the long aisle. If you're lucky, you have a job that sends you home each day drained of all urge to reflect upon your life. If you're very lucky indeed, you are so exhausted that you don't lie awake asking yourself the musical question *Is that all there is?* over and over through sleepless hours, repeating yourself only partly because that's the only line of the song you know.

Louisa found me at the staff room kitchen sink.

"Right. Let's get you on track. Friday you were a zombie with an invigorating wake-up car accident. Today, we do something about this droopy-underwear career of yours."

I was washing up the usual mystery collection of somebody else's dirty dishes while brooding on my inability to convince my kindergarten student Sammy to come out from under the art table and on Sammy's mother's inability to stop phoning the school to complain about it. I was almost glad when Louisa dragged me away from the sink and into the hallway, where she always supposed there was more privacy despite the open classroom doors behind which sat hundreds of kids who would listen to anything rather than their teachers.

"Some of those forks have been in the sink since June," I told her, but Louisa never cared what you said as long as you listened to her.

She hauled me farther down the corridor. "You say you need opportunities to work outside of the narrow confines of your classroom. There's a new band sub."

"I don't want to teach band, Louisa."

"I'm talking about mentorship opportunities. The old leading the young. Also, he's like the Grand Canyon. You shouldn't miss him."

"I've seen the Grand Canyon, Louisa." I cracked one of the double doors to the multi and staggered out into the band class on the other side of the door, propelled by a shove from Louisa, who I would now, on top of all my other pressing responsibilities, have to kill.

The whole room of Grade 7s, along with their redheaded young teacher, stopped in the middle of the 'Surprise Symphony' and stared at me.

"Are you the surprise?" Norman, Louisa's tallest and most big-mouthed student, asked.

"A pleasant surprise," the band sub said, apparently to put me at my ease.

"Oh, hi," I said. "Sorry to interrupt … I want some, er, strings for my school guitar, but I'll come back later. You sound good, everybody."

The kids and I smiled at each other, for although they were twelve years old now, not long ago they had been my five-year-old kindergarten students, singing along while I strummed 'Baby Beluga', and they would be dear to me forever. Norman, on alto sax, let out a low note that sounded perilously close to a fart. Lovely Norman, I thought, may you never change.

"Norman, I think you know what you did," the band teacher said.

Norman stood up and hung his head. He folded his band chair and walked sadly past me in big Grade 7 sneakers.

"I know, I know," he muttered. "One toot and I'm oot."

"Certainly not." I sized up the new band teacher as beautiful but cruel. I stared him down. "It was my fault entirely, bursting in here in the middle of your class. If anyone should be oot, it's me."

"I'm establishing discipline," the band sub said. "The first thing they teach you is not to let the woodwind section get out of control."

I said coldly, "You must be kind to all sections of the orchestra."

I backed out through the doors, followed by the sound of applause from the band. Louisa, chortling, led me back towards the staff room.

"Just as I told you, there are new educational experiences for you to explore here at Westside Elementary, along with opportunities to take a leadership role, as we've both just witnessed. You won't get anything better in administration. And you won't get anything better at Central."

She'd made her point. And, fortunately, one unexpected benefit you receive when you pass forty is an easy assumption of dignity. From up here on the high shelf of life's experience, I would be kind to the new band sub. I would be cool. I would be his teaching colleague, Susan Sarandon. I would be so cool he'd see his breath in the air around me.

Furthermore, maybe Louisa and Julia were correct, and I should take on a greater leadership role in my home school. In this way I could train myself for a move into a management role someday, when and if I felt ready. I could sign up for lunch-bag reflection meetings right here at Westside. I might direct school concerts. In time, perhaps, I would outgrow my beloved kindergarten classroom, and an administration role would overtake me like an alien pod fungus, changing me in ways I couldn't now imagine, until transformation became complete and irreversible.

Chapter 3

I was usually delighted to attend the teachers' pub on Friday afternoons. I enjoyed the Guinness situation, and as well there was the sight of joyful teachers gambolling about the open portal to the weekend. However, on the Friday after the Zombie Walk, the Sammy situation was wearing me out, and I begged off.

Louisa was having none of it.

"You're not too tired," she argued. "You are just old, and a pint will set you right." She sat us at a half-empty table and went to find us some.

The pub buzzed happily, and my friend Bruce plunked his beer down on my table. He swung his long frame into the captain's chair across from me.

I asked him how it was going.

"Fine," he groaned.

Poor Bruce. I usually thought of him as *poor Bruce*, although sometimes he was *that bugger Bruce*. You must understand that during the year I was getting my courage up to leave my marriage, Bruce was separated from his wife and a big cheerleader for the single life.

"Why are you staying?" he would demand. "You know you're going to move out like I did. Come on, be a man. I'll be here for you."

Bruce had appealing brown eyes, and it was nice to think that there was going to be somebody to meet me at the airport, so to speak, when I deplaned from marriage. And then the very week I left my husband, Bruce went back to his wife.

"Good God," I asked him. "What happened? Did you fall in love again, TV-style?"

He said no, Jeanette still hated him, but they'd decided to stick together for the kids. It was a five-year plan.

This five-year plan was the kind of cuckoo idea that could only have been developed by two high school counsellors who hated each other. The plan was no sex for five years, raise the four kids, and then split.

Bruce thought their plan was brilliant.

"I can do five years with no sex, no problem," he'd told me the day he'd moved back in with Jeanette. Celibacy was no bar to his happiness, he said, because he played guitar and planned to spend the five years expressing himself through music whenever any sexual urge came over him. I was sure he was sincere, but he tended to stare at my breasts a lot.

"I'm going to do it, Hay," he said. "I'm going to start up a band."

"Perfect," I said. "Tell me when your gigs are and I'll come."

"I'm going to need a rhythm guitarist," he told me.

"Oh." I dabbed at a puddle of beer on the table and wished I had any real talent. "Well, you could ask Jason. He's good." Jason, like Bruce, played brilliantly and knew the words to every blues and rock song you ever heard, even early B-sides recorded decades before he was born.

Bruce shook his head. "I don't want a lead guitar player. I'm a lead guitar player. What I need is a rhythm guitarist to hold the whole thing together when I'm taking solos. No fancy stuff. I need someone to be the lettuce in the salad."

"Well, maybe Jason would play rhythm," I said.

"I was thinking maybe you'd do it." Bruce stirred his beer with his finger.

I stared at him. Was he crazy? Bruce wasn't some armchair musician, backing up Ed Sheeran on speaker in his rec room. Bruce really played, in venues sometimes, and was so good that he would wear just any old T-shirt on stage.

"Bruce, I stink."

He glared at me. "Stop that. I've jammed with you, and you do not stink. Listen, when you're putting together a band, you've got to have people who can get along with you and who can do their job. You know all the chords, right?"

"Yes," I said. I'd played guitar since I was twelve.

"And you've got a good rock groove."

"Yes." Jason had taught me.

"And you can sing harmony," he said.

"Yes," I lied.

I was in a band.

Of course, you must love my job to do it. You can't take or leave teaching, you must love it with an unreasonable passion or you'll be driven mad within hours by the constant ebb and flow of twenty-odd small people, each with a different agenda. Without the invisible shield of your affection for kids, how could you bear the tattling, the crying, and above all, the jokes? If you don't love those children, you'd be better off in any other job in the world. You'd do better to put on a miner's hat and descend into dark caverns; you'd be happier wearing an orange hat frying up fast food; you'd be better off — this was my personal nightmare — selling unnecessary personal items door-to-door on commission. But I expected, indeed hoped, to teach kindergarten until I died.

Not that I didn't buy lottery tickets. But I did love the kids — even the whiners, the line-budgers, and the ones like Sammy who wouldn't come out from under the table no matter how intriguing the lesson. I even found a way to love the kids who would rip the paper off the walls if you turned your back on them. Which, on this warm late September morning, was exactly what Corey was doing.

I had spent an hour the day before putting up that bulletin board. It was a thing of relative beauty, with new orange paper stapled up behind lovingly matted paintings of colourful if unrecognizable objects. The title, cut out in wobbly but sincere green letters, read *Little Artists with Big Ideas*. Louisa always said my bulletin boards resembled nothing so much as the abandoned campaigns of failed ad men. Corey, humming a happy little song, ripped a band of orange paper off the wall.

Julia walked in, wearing her usual administrative calm. "Hayley, I have something of the utmost importance regarding your professional development ..."

"Hi!" Corey grinned at us from his perch on the window ledge. Some children would have greeted their teacher and principal with a significant lack of joy when discovered ripping apart a bulletin board, but not Corey. His brown eyes gleamed behind his glasses, and with his little tuft of yellow hair and bright sweatshirt he resembled a small tropical bird, the kind that lives on bugs and fruit in the rainforest. He pulled a strip of the orange paper longways down the edge of my bulletin board, and then tore it another foot or so crosswise, a slow, careful motion that he performed with his eyes up close to the tear. He jumped off the ledge, the end of my orange paper still in his hand. A rending noise accompanied his descent, and as he landed on sensibly bent knees, his arms out with the grace of a successful gymnast, six paintings by Little Artists flopped to the ground, and all my display library books toppled across the ledge.

A sudden cry turned my attention to the playhouse area. Leslie and Jaz dashed toward us. Leslie picked up a painting from the floor and cradled it in her arms. "Oh, my lovely, lovely picture," she mourned.

Jaz leaned in for a closer look. "That's *my* picture," she cried.

"Lovely, lovely," Leslie sobbed.

I turned away from Julia and put my arm around Leslie. "Now, Corey," I told him. "You didn't mean to make Leslie sad, I know that, but she is sad, and maybe there's something you need to say to her that will make her feel better."

Corey bent down and peered at Leslie's wet face. "Don't feel bad, Leslie, it wasn't so good a picture."

Julia took me by the arm and led me a few feet away. "Hayley, you're a superb teacher, and I'm beginning to think that's part of your problem. What if you began work towards an administrative role? Vice-principal? There will soon be an opening across town at Eastside Elementary."

With my arms full of ripped orange backing paper, I joked, "Right now I feel more like a custodian."

"That's a proud calling, too." Julia took the paper from me, deposited it into the recycling box, and escorted Corey off to the water table where he could develop his grasp of the conservation of water in variously shaped receptacles, as in Piaget's studies; she propelled Leslie and Jaz towards the painting easels in order that they might restock the world of art. I took the attendance folder from Eejin as she held it out to me and reported, "Sammy's under the table again."

Somebody knocked on the open door. Sammy's mother leaned into the room, Sammy's baby brother in her arms. In his mouth he held what looked like the ear of a large pink stuffed rabbit.

I thought, *hell.* I try to keep an open line of communication with my class parents—the more prevalent, sliced-fruit-bearing sort as well as the rare damned annoying ones. But, every morning since September the third, I hoped above all things on heaven and earth that Sammy's mother would take his three siblings and go home without noticing that he had crawled under that table again.

"Oh, Mrs Andersen!" Sammy's mother called. She held the baby in her arms while her toddlers peered up at me from between her knees.

"*Ms* Andersen." I held my attendance folder over my vital organs. "Hayley, if you like."

"Sammy has taken my cell phone. Will you get it, please?"

"Students are not allowed to have cell phones," Julia explained from the painting area. "It's school policy."

"Well, exactly," Mrs Halter said.

There was another knock at the door. Two more of my parents squeezed in past Mrs Halter — Arzee's dad and Carney's mom, my two most helpful parents.

Arzee's dad pushed a bag full of yogurt containers with lids for our painting centre into my arms, and on top of them Carney's mom balanced a big red bowl of sliced oranges for snack. I tumbled the lot onto my desk, marked Eejin and Ralph present, and tried to care about Mrs Halter's bloody cell phone.

"Ms Andersen," Mrs Halter repeated, "I need the cell phone, if you wouldn't mind." The baby leaned across her breast and reached for the orange segments. "This incident is one of many, and I've had some talks with your principal about your rationale for keeping my child under the table."

"It's not unusual for children to find quiet spaces when they begin school, and he'll come out when he's comfortable with the group."

It was circle time. It was past time for circle time. I squatted down and spotted Sammy's shoes at the back under the library table.

A little song played under the table. Sammy was receiving a text.

I turned to his mother. "I'll tell you what: I'll get the phone from him later and leave it in my box in the office."

"All right," Mrs Halter said. "But it's highly inconvenient."

"Can you please make sure he doesn't bring the phone anymore?" I asked Mrs Halter. "It really is against the rules for students to bring phones to school."

Louisa's Grade 7 student Norman hip-hopped into the room, a cell phone pressed to his ear. He wore the air of a businessman on a tight schedule. He said, "I heard the kid who lives under the table brought his phone into class, and Louisa said it was the thin edge of the wedge." Louisa's kids all called her by her first name. It was iconoclastic and liberal-minded, and Julia hated it, which was why Louisa insisted on it. Norman leaned down and shouted toward Sammy's feet. "Hey, table boy! Rock on!"

"Table boy?" Mrs Halter took an orange quarter away from her baby, put it back into the communal bowl, and delivered a hard look to Norman.

"Don't call Sammy 'table boy', Norman," I said. "And hand over your phone."

He handed it to me. "Sure, Ms Andersen, it's for you. It's Louisa, phoning from the classroom. She says we can all phone now; we're muscling through the twenty-first century, and the school's going to allow open use of cell phones and chewing gum."

"Gum!" I'd been teaching for a long time, and I hated all gum.

"Gum chewing seems a minor problem to me," Mrs Halter said, "when you can't provide my child with a learning environment comfortable and attractive enough to encourage him to come out from under a table to join the class." Her arm curved protectively about her younger child. She seemed to me about ready to cry.

Julia addressed her with ineffable kindness. "Come, let me give you a cup of coffee in the staff room."

Sammy's mother left wearing a look I tried to find unreadable, but the baby waved its pink bunny ear affably.

If I were a vice-principal, I could give parents coffee instead of taking Mrs Halter's critiques on the chin. I said into the phone, "Louisa, when I am a vice-principal, I will ensure that there is no gum chewing anywhere in the world."

At the other end of the connection, Louisa snapped her gum. "You'll never be a vice-principal."

"How would you know that?" I demanded.

"Because you'd be miserable out of your classroom, slumming it in administration. The school board will transfer you to another school without even asking me if I want to be here alone. So don't fall into Julia's trap."

"What am I, a mouse? There's no trap, Louisa. She thinks I'd be a good administrator."

"Well, you need a master's degree to be a vice-principal, and you don't have one."

"I do so have one."

"*How* can you be so secretive? You're like a thief in the night," Louisa growled. "Hey, do you want some earthworms? I've got an aquarium full here, perfect for a kindergarten room. What do you say?"

"Louisa, I already told you I don't want your earthworms."

"Perfect pets, so why not?"

"Because even though they are God's creatures, they creep me out."

"You mouse. Well then, you got any red construction paper?"

"You can have it if you swallow your gum."

I gave Norman back the phone and pointed him towards my paper cupboard. Then I ticked off names on the register. "Sammy's under the table. I don't see Matthew or Jonathan. Anyone else away?"

Waving matching red-and-black backpacks around their heads and shouting, "It's pizza day!" Matthew and Jonathan bowled into the classroom. They compensated for not being born identical twins by doing everything together, at the same time and at the top of their lungs. This morning both were also liberally spattered with mud. I reminded myself to have a word with the class about staying away from the muddy area of the playground, after which I would try to convince dogs not to want bones.

"Pizza, pizza!" Kyler joined Matthew and Jonathan, and the three of them jumped up and down, their little synapses crackling back and forth so wildly that, for them, everything else in the world except their pizza dance ceased to exist. I reached out to the little bell on my desk, ready to ring for quiet. But, from beneath the table at the back of the room, I caught sight of two bright eyes in the shadows. Sammy watched the little boys together as they danced in friendship across the classroom carpet.

I left the bell alone. I knew how it could be to dance like Kyler, Matthew, and Jonathan. These days, I felt more like Sammy.

Thursday. After school. Before Bruce's band practice. I couldn't cancel his fine offer by text, so I phoned him. I had to lean against my kitchen counter to stand upright, and my hands shook, but inside I felt free, and lighter. In fact, I was a free, light coward to whom such a fantastic and undeserved musical opportunity would never come again. It was a wonderful sensation.

"Hayley?" I heard Bruce say.

I swallowed. He would be disappointed, of course, yet deep inside he had to know — no matter how much he liked me and my breasts as friends — that I was not a real musician. When you speak the truth it is easy to find the words, and so it was that they flowed from my mouth, clear and sweet as spring water and ringing with rightness.

"Bruce, I'm sorry, but I can't be in the band."

There was a pause. I heard a faint tapping from the other end of the line, as of a guitar pick against a tabletop.

"Bruce? I'm out. I can't do it. You're going to have to find someone who can sing."

"Hello?" he said again, a little louder. "Hayley?"

"Bruce, I'm not good enough to be able to —"

"Is anyone there?" Bruce said. "Dammit, I can't hear a thing. Is this an obscene call? Shouldn't you be breathing or something?"

"Hell," I muttered. "Never mind."

"Right," he grunted. "See you at seven, Hayley."

Guitar and amp in hand, I trundled down the narrow corridor past the elevator, which was out of order, towards my building's stairway. There I met Deirdre from the apartment below mine. I swung the amp out of her way, and it bashed against my butt. She angled her bosom around me and shot me a narrow, thickly eye-shadowed frown over her shoulder. In good conscience, I couldn't blame Deirdre for giving me a dirty look, equipped as I was with musical items that, if plugged in and turned up high, would rattle the walls and murder her sleep. As well, a certain lifestyle was associated with musicians. What, my neighbour Deirdre might have asked herself, was to stop me from practising Zeppelin solos early on Sunday mornings? Would she find bearded drummers bouncing against her doorway at midnight and calling for weed? I imagined myself keeping musicians' hours, stumbling home drunk with a trumpet player at three on a work night, tooting and reeling along the hall. The notion sustained me as I drove to Richmond and lugged my guitar and amp into Bruce's garage. I set them down on the unmarked concrete floor next to his workbench.

Bruce tossed me a binder. "It's a bunch of classic blues numbers I put together from my old set books and lyrics sites. If you look at the back, you can see I've got them cross-indexed by artist and title."

"And colour-coded, alphabetized tabs," I noted. It would have been so much easier to put together on our school tablets. "A lot of late nights on your own, Bruce?"

Bruce snorted good-naturedly, and the bass player walked in with the drummer.

"These guys are insanely good," Bruce told me in a low voice, then called out to them, "Hey, Giorgio. Hey, Ray. This is Hayley."

Giorgio, the drummer, looked me up and down. "Hayley, eh? I see you're a girl."

Ray took his set book from Bruce and smacked Giorgio across the top of his curly head with it. "Sorry, we don't see a lot of girl band members. And Giorgio hardly sees a girl at all. Are you keyboards?"

"Or tambourine?" Giorgio cracked his gum.

"Triangle?" Ray asked.

Bruce put a hand on my arm. "She has a 1 9 6 9 Gibson sunburst on her lap, so show her a little respect, will you? She's rhythm and backup vocals, and I asked her before I asked you guys, all right?"

"Yeah, yeah," Giorgio said.

Bruce said to me, "Don't fear them. They like to piss people off."

Ray grinned. "Yeah, because nobody ever fired a bass player."

"The Beatles did," Bruce pointed out. "They fired Stuart—"

"Stuart quit," Ray corrected him.

"Yeah, yeah," Giorgio said. He snapped his snare stand down in front of the workbench. "And nobody ever fired a solid drummer like myself either. Watch me go back out to the car to get my drum kit and notice the swagger in my walk. And how all of you drop everything and come help me."

We helped him carry his kit, Ray swearing mightily at every step, and then plugged in our own guitars and tested for sound levels. In front of my amp, Bruce had set up a microphone adjusted with precision to the exact elevation of my mouth. Here it loomed: my own microphone. I ran my damp palm over the blue plastic cover of the set binder and tried to feel grateful.

"Check, check," I said into the mesh of the mic. I jumped as my voice bounced back at me from the monitor speaker on the floor by the garage door. For a moment I forgot to breathe.

"What you got for us, Brucie?" The ceiling light reflected off Ray's dome of a head. He yawned. "What have you got for this co-ed band?"

"I want to start with 'Hey, Baby'," Bruce told us. "The songs are listed alphabetically, and you'll see that it's on page twelve."

Giorgio broke into an unrequested drum solo that caused me to drop my jaw. I looked at him with his curly black hair, Pearl drum kit, and 1988 AC/DC *Blow Up Your Video* tour T-shirt, then jumped as Ray scuttled a scale up and down the neck of his Stingray bass, about ten notes to a heartbeat. I turned down the volume on my amp.

"It's in D," Bruce told us.

Ray rolled his eyes. "Bruce, I've been playing 'Hey, Baby' since I was one year old. Let's go."

Giorgio banged his sticks together hard, twice, and I hit a D, which sounded, thank the gods, exactly like a real D. Bruce held his hand up to stop us.

"I know you know it, Ray and Giorgio, but I want to make sure the rest of us are okay on the harmonies."

The harmonies. I blinked rapidly, then, with an effort, relaxed my face into an open, listening expression as might be worn by Adele while rehearsing a new tune in the key of D, with harmonies.

"Got it."

"Yeah." Ray shrugged. "You come in on the A, I'll come in on the D, and Hayley hits the F-sharp. No problemo. Hit it, Giorgio."

Giorgio hit his sticks, then threw them up into the air as Bruce again held his hand up to bring the song to a halt. I jumped as the drumsticks clattered to the ground. It occurred to me that if Giorgio walked out on the band right now, I would be able, without apologies to Bruce or to myself, to pack up my equipment, drive home, and crawl safely into bed forever. If Giorgio or Ray walked, then we had a situation in which it wasn't me who blew the only chance that a talentless classroom hack would ever have to play in a real band.

I picked up the drumsticks and handed them back to Giorgio.

"Sorry, Ray." Bruce hoisted his Les Paul around his shoulders. "I wasn't ready, and traditionally, as founder and lead guitarist, I should say, 'Let's go', all right?"

"Fine," Ray said. "So let's go."

Giorgio clacked his sticks again. We all started in. I adjusted the crunch on my amp and looked up to see Bruce wagging his guitar neck at me and at the microphone. My microphone.

I stepped up to it while Bruce sang his 'hey' on A. I breathed hard. Ray came in with his "Hey," on D. And now here it was.

I was supposed to come in with a harmony on the first 'hey' with an F-sharp.

Damned if I could find F-sharp anywhere in my throat.

They all looked at me. And they all looked away. I didn't sing for the rest of practice.

"I'm sorry," I told Bruce when we were winding up the cords.

I waited for him to say that it hadn't worked out, that he would have to find a new singer. A confident singer. A singer, in short, who could sing.

But he gave my shoulder a squeeze and carried my amp out to the car for me.

CHAPTER 4

At ten past three, Apollo leaned into my classroom. "That's enough gloom from you, Ms Andersen. We're going to the movies, where we will banish all your troubles."

Going with Apollo to the movies had often cheered me. In the hard grey days towards the end of my marriage, when Ken had done nothing but sit at his computer, Apollo took me to see classic indie films. He ate Nibs for hours at my side while we endured countless scenes of unbearable physical and emotional suffering — scenes like the one at the end of *Exotica* where you see a nice house and a cat on the front porch, but you know that behind the door lies spiritual torment. Whenever I went to the movies with Apollo, I always staggered out at the end, shaken yet inexplicably cheered by two hours spent plumbing the depths of human suffering. For Apollo, the more agonizing and obscure the film, the better he liked it. We always went to this great repertory theatre, the Kits, that had low prices and unbelievably uncomfortable seats. You had to scrootch down so that your lower back was curved into the seat and your rear end stuck out into the air. It was hardly ever crowded there, so you could usually find a good spot. I liked it up front, where the screen became the entire world, the way it might be in your space capsule as you approached the moon: big, bright, and everywhere. Apollo never moved out of the back row. He would always say, "It hurts my eyes to sit up front." I happened to know the real reason he sat at the back, because he'd told me the first time we caught a show together. He'd received a hand job in the back row of a movie theatre when he was eighteen, and the memory added to the whole viewing experience.

Since I'd never had anything happen to me in the front row of a theatre except putting my foot into a puddle of cola, I had to sit at the back when we went together. However, the films were always interesting: there was a black-and-white Hungarian one about a bathhouse falling down, and another one, also black and white, where a nun gets walled into a church. She spends most of the film walled in. I figure it cost about $49.99 to make that one if they didn't have to buy the bricks.

Apollo and I really liked the nun movie because there was a flash of red three-quarters of the way through, a kind of red flame that only lasted for a second. We could never figure out what it meant. Only those viewers who had not dozed off while the villagers brought bread and milk to the nun in her cell would have caught this flash of red. This made us feel we were acute and penetrating moviegoers. Apollo decided the red flash was her passion, her religious passion that only God could see, so that for a scarlet instant we took God's perspective. He said the reason the flash was so short was that it goes on forever in the eternal now, and because each life is ephemeral and eternal at the same time. All this, and admission was half price midweek.

I met Apollo at the theatre that Wednesday night. The film was going to be in Russian, and he'd insisted it would be so gloomy that it would evoke in me an almost unbearable optimism.

"Hey, Apollo." I slumped down next to him. "I see you're sitting in the back row again. Still hoping, eh?"

He grinned at me from beneath the brim of his baseball cap. "I have no idea what you mean."

An usher came by and asked Apollo to take off his cap.

"Why should you have to take it off?" I asked. "Life is so unfair."

"It's true, nobody's fair to the bald," Apollo said. "Next they'll tell comb-overers to comb back down."

I scowled at the usher's back. "Do you realize that baseball caps have almost entirely replaced comb-overs? In fact, it's time we show our appreciation as a civilization."

"Yes, the hour has come."

"I believe we should get rid of the word *bald* and replace it with *baseball cap*. You are not bald, you are a baseball cap guy, and furthermore, I think that bald — I mean baseball cap men — look exactly as handsome as if they did have hair."

"Jason Statham," Apollo said fiercely.

"I say, let all of you wear your baseball caps everywhere you want to."

"In fancy restaurants."

"Swimming, and to bed with new lovers. I have a theory that baldness —"

"Baseball cap-icity."

"— is an imagined handicap in men who date after thirty. But I think it's simply another kind of hair: blond hair, black hair, no hair."

"Let's not forget other imagined handicaps," Apollo said broodingly. "Like having kids. But really, if somebody likes you, he will go out with you and your kids too, and put up with outrageous expressions of jealousy and resentment and abuse from them, even when they pull the baseball cap off your bald head and play Frisbee with it."

I nodded. Apollo was beginning to sound less philosophical and more autobiographical. "Your latest?"

"He remains to be seen. But I didn't get candy to cheer myself up." Apollo ripped open a bag of red liquorice and held it out to me. "In some ways I see your life in that film, *The Young Poisoner's Handbook*, when the kid brought everyone coffee and you couldn't tell which mug had the arsenic in it."

"You mean because you never know whether a day will bring joy or sorrow?"

Apollo pressed more red liquorice upon me. "No, what I mean is that in the same way the mug was pure untainted porcelain, made deadly only by the arsenic inside it, so too every day is rendered good or bad by what *we put into it*. You see?"

We scrootched even lower. Apollo put his cap back on.

"I am heartbroken," I explained to the brim of his cap. "I failed at having a happy marriage, and I'm still failing at being happy getting out of a sad one."

Apollo took my hand and poured the remaining red liquorice into it. "I didn't realize you still wanted to be part of a couple. If that's how you want to improve your lot in life, there are lots of divorced guys your age out there."

"It's the last thing I'm looking for." But I tried out the idea of a divorced man my age, rolling up his sprinkler hose outside his garage. It was a meaningless exercise, and Apollo knew as well as I did what a divorced man my age really wanted: a twenty-two-year-old who didn't wear underwear.

The lights went down, and the Cyrillic titles went up. I said, "How pleasant it would be to wall myself into a church like that nun in the movie. Villagers would bring bread and ask for advice."

"Here's some advice for your walled-up self: get free. Be a villager."

"Leave everything, you mean?" I asked. "But I don't want to leave my school and my friends."

"I'd sure miss you."

If I left what I loved, where would I go? "Cheer me up, Apollo. You promised."

"So I did." Apollo folded his arms across his middle. "This had better be a really depressing movie."

Thursday night at practice in Bruce's garage, Ray snapped his patch cord into his bass and jerked his thumb at me.

"You ought to get drunk," he said.

"Why?" Giorgio asked. "Aside from everybody should get drunk."

"No, they shouldn't all get drunk," Bruce argued. "Not everybody."

"Everybody," Giorgio said.

Bruce unplugged a drill press from his garage workbench and plugged his amp into the socket. "Not little children, not alcoholics, not people who are driving."

Giorgio snorted. "You are both obvious and pussy in your reasoning. I was speaking on a worldwide scale: everyone should be drunk."

I stared at Giorgio with new respect. He was a man with a world view. "You mean like if everyone were drunk, there wouldn't be wars? We'd all get along, arms looped over each other's shoulders, walking in peace, singing Beatles songs together?"

Giorgio smiled blandly. "Yeah, like that."

"I don't mean just to get her to sing," Ray said. "I think we should happify her up."

"You pig," Giorgio said in a high voice. "Anyway, you're married."

"We're all *married*," Ray grunted.

"I'm not," I told him.

"Don't brag," Giorgio said. "No one likes a drunken braggart."

"I'm not drunk." I set down my can of Guinness. "In fact, I think I'm never getting drunk again."

Giorgio crossed his drumsticks at me as if I had stood up and witnessed for Satan.

"I have to make changes," I said.

Ray ignored me. "If we get her drunk, not only will she cheer up, but maybe she'll lose all her inhibitions and sing."

"See, that's what I mean. Everybody should lose all their inhibitions," Giorgio said, who as far as I could see retained only enough inhibitions to appear clothed in public. He fitted his snare into its stand, twisted the nuts underneath, raised the height of the drum by an inch, then dropped it down again with a thump.

Maybe Ray was right, and a few beers would help me get up the courage to sing—or to walk out on the band forever. I eyed the cooler. Lots of musicians used drink or drugs to help them stand up in front of a crowd. This was accepted practice. I imagined myself standing at the microphone, loose and lubricated with spirits, singing like a fallen angel. Ray and Giorgio would swallow every rude word they'd ever said about my harmonies and clap me on the back. Bruce would be so proud of me. And when you got right down to it, anybody could sing. My kindergarten students could sing. I looked at the microphone on its stand in front of me, so shiny and amplifiable, and shuddered.

Bruce studied me with the insightful eye of the high-school counsellor. "Too many beers may act as a depressant. Anyhow, I don't think we'll need to take any heroic measures here, because Hayley promised that she'd sing tonight. Didn't you, Hayley?"

"Didn't I what?" I found myself all at once busy with my B string, which wanted to be a little bit sharp.

Bruce coughed. "You're going to sing today, right?"

I sat on my amp with my arms and legs crossed to keep them still.

Giorgio leaned back on his drum stool and stuck out his gut. "Kick her out if she won't sing. No offence, Hayley, but rhythm guitarists are a dime a dozen."

"You're wrong," Bruce said. "Rhythm guitarists who have no ambition to play lead guitar are gold. Listen, Hay, it's just the four of us. Step up to the mic and sing."

I eyed the microphone. "Why do I have to sing, anyway? You sing great, Bruce. All three of you can sing. You don't need me to sing. I'm in the band to be the lettuce in the salad, while you guys are the special vegetables."

"I bags avocado," Giorgio said.

"Fucking prima donna," Ray said. "Not you, Hayley. I think I'm more avocado. And you, Giorgio, are more like a cherry tomato."

"Not since I was fifteen," Giorgio retorted.

Bruce said, "Hayley, you've got to sing in the band. Otherwise it's stupid to have a girl in the band. Everybody will be waiting to hear you sing and when you don't, they'll all be disappointed."

"They'll be disappointed if I do sing." But I stood and sidled up to the mic. I blew into it. "Check, check."

"I can't believe you don't sing with your kindergarten kids," Ray said.

I told him I sang with my class.

"Well, do they cry, or does anybody's head explode?"

"Shut up, Ray," Bruce said.

"Safety check," the bass player explained.

"I want to be prawns at least," Giorgio said. "Prawns are good in a salad. Or crab."

"Hay, what do you want to sing?" Bruce said patiently. He wasn't a school counsellor for nothing. "Whatever you want, Hay."

I grimaced. I was not a professional singer. I had never claimed to be one, except for that moment in the bar with Bruce when I'd lied my way into his band. But it seemed that my doom had arrived. I looked over at Bruce and caught his eye. He believed in me.

Life at its darkest is often transactional. I would have to sing for Bruce.

§

Look for the novel Younger Men *coming in 2026 from Pulp Literature Press.*

Also by Mel Anastasiou

THE EXTRA: A MONUMENT STUDIOS MYSTERY

Vancouver schoolmarm Frankie Ray runs away to Silver Screen Hollywood to test her conviction that an actress who lacks glamour but has talent and an enterprising attitude can make it in the movies. But when a dissolute, womanizing matinee idol turns up dead on her sofa, Frankie's career hopes shatter. She'll need all her acting chops to sleuth out the murderer and clear her name.

STELLA RYMAN AND THE FAIRMOUNT MANOR MYSTERIES

On this particular sun-and-shade April morning at Fairmount Manor, Stella Ryman no more entertained the idea of becoming an amateur sleuth than she did of entering next spring's Boston Marathon. For not only was Stella eighty-two years old, but she had lately sold her home and a lifetime of gathered possessions and washed up at Fairmount Manor Care Home in such a state that she would have bet her remaining seven pairs of socks that she'd be dead in half a year.

THE LABOURS OF MRS STELLA RYMAN:
FURTHER FAIRMOUNT MANOR MYSTERIES

When the machineries of institution fail to protect Fairmount Manor, octogenarian amateur sleuth Mrs Stella Ryman rolls up her fleece jacket sleeves to protect Fairmount from a thief, investigate a gun-toting resident, set right a mishandled investigation of a man's death, pursue spectres and footpads walking at midnight, and discover Thelma Hu's long-lost fortune. No good deed goes unpunished, though, and Stella will face struggles, mysteries, and sacrifices that hit her where she lives.

PULPLITERATURE.COM

THE ARTISTS

Jenn Ashton
Cover artist, Surfacing

Jenn Ashton is an award-winning Squamish author, visual artist, and filmmaker. Her book of short stories, *People Like Frank, and Other Stories from The Edge of Normal* (Tidewater Press, 2020) was a finalist for the 2021 Indigenous Voices Award, and her short story 'Hungry' won in 2024. Jenn is an authenticity reader for Penguin/Random House USA, where she completed work on *Killers of the Flower Moon,* and she also works for Knopf Doubleday and Cengage Canada. When she is not writing, painting, or teaching, she enjoys cedar and wool weaving, making regalia, and watching short films. She currently studies history at the University of Edinburgh.

About *Surfacing,* she says, "The painting was part of my personal reconciliation process of coming home to my S̲k̲w̲x̲wú7mesh First Nation community. As a result of residential schools, my family lost their culture, and I was raised on the outside. Over the past two decades, my family and I have come home, and this process resulted in many different creative expressions through art and writing."

Helena Pantsis
Illustrator, 'Sick Pay'

A long-time writer and storyteller, Helena Pantsis recently found her calling in comics when she became burnt out from the stress of juggling work, illness, and creative pursuits, all in the very limited hours that come in a day. Returning to her childhood love of drawing, she realized that the habit was something that could be adapted to involve her love of play, art, writing, and experimentalism.

'Sick Pay' is where her stressors become the motivation for her art. Exploring the pressures of capitalism, the drain of chronic illness, and the dedication to an art form which, in its joyful, childish origins, is the antithesis of these things, Pantsis attempts to encapsulate the body-depleting experience of the incessant working life.

Helena is a strong advocate for the act of making simply for the love of it, often collaborating with poets to bring their words to life in drawing, and platforming writers whose work doesn't fit elsewhere in *Going Down Swinging*, the journal she co-edits in Naarm, Australia. She champions the strange, the hybrid, the uncategorizable, and that which falls between the bounds, always looking to devour whatever happens to suit her ever-changing appetite.

Mel Anastasiou

In-house illustrator

Mel Anastasiou loves drawing for *Pulp Literature* because she loves the stories she illustrates. She draws in black and white, working from imagination and inspired by details from Renaissance compositions. You can find illustrations, writing tips, and news about her books and novellas at melanastasiou.wordpress.com, and see more of her artwork on Facebook at Bird and Branch Artwork.

HALL OF FAME

These are the heroes — the Patrons and Pulp Literati whose monthly support helped bring you this issue. Please lift your glasses and give them a rousing cheer!

The Brewers
Dana Tye Rally

The Innkeepers
Abigail Bruce
Andrea Kepple
David Jensen
Ev Bishop
Gillian Gardiner
Kevin Harris
Lorna Ens
Mark Francis
Richard Ohnemus
Robin McGillveray
Susan Jackson
Kevin S Moul

The Cicerones
Bjarne Hansen
Jennifer Sommersby
Roger & Anne Anastasiou
Zoë Ricard

The Bartenders
Alana Krider
Andrea Kirkham
Anna Belkine
Brighton Hugg
Bryan Moose
Cheryl Andrichuk
Chris Olee
Dave Wayne
Deepthi Atukorala
Dena Linn Chen
Devan Erno
Ernst Pulido
Evelyn Ann
Finnian Burnett
Hannah Moor
James Carlino
Jennifer Getsinger
Jillian Shoichet
Kat Hankinson
Kate Johnson
Katherine Derbyshire
kc dyer

Kelsey Brennan
Kim Seary
KT Wagner
Leny Wagner
Lin & John Richardson
Margot Landels
Margot Spronk
Megan Shaw
Michelle Balfour
Mike Sylvester
Peter Halasz
Rapscallion
Regina Rogers
Richard Gropp
Ron Graves
Scott F Gray
Shannon Saunders
Star
Suzanne Philip
Venasa Simpson

The Regulars

Adam Fout
Alice Rhoades
Andy W
BC
Brandi Estey-Burtt
Catherine Levinson
Charity Tahmaseb
Christopher Bridgen
Emmy Bee
Jenny Blackford
JS Andrew
Marilyn Holt
Marilyn K
Marta Salek
Meredith Frazier
Michelle Robinson
Peter Darbyshire
Rina Piccolo
Vera

If you would like to join the ranks of these worthies, you can become a patron on Patreon at patreon.com/pulplit or join the Pulp Literati through our website at pulpliterature.com/join-pulp-literati.

ARC **POETRY**

Canada's poetry magazine for over 45 years

3 issues per year, in
Spring, Summer,
and Fall
$40 for one year
$65 for two years*
subscribe online at
arcpoetry.ca

*Subscription rates listed for Canadian subscribers

 @ Arc Poetry Magazine 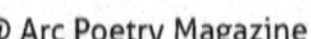  @ arcpoetrymag

The Malahat Review
ESSENTIAL POETRY · FICTION · CREATIVE NONFICTION

$35 fee
enter by Nov. 1

Open Season Awards

$6000 prize money in three categories

- poetry
- short fiction
- creative nonfiction

Commit these deadlines to memory

February 1, 2026
Novella Prize | $2000
One writer gets the prize

May 1, 2026
Far Horizons Award for Poetry | $1250
One writer gets the prize

August 1, 2026
Constance Rooke Creative Nonfiction Prize | $1250
One writer gets the prize

malahatreview.ca
malahat@uvic.ca

University of Victoria

Join us in Penticton for the 2025

Wine Country Writers' Festival

Friday, September 26:
Opening Night Gala at Linden Gardens, including
hors d'ouevres, a selection of wine and other beverages, and
readings by all our features writers

Saturday, September 27:
A jam-packed day of literary events at Okanagan College
(Penticton Campus):

* Keynote speech by Carleigh Baker
* Cross-genre workshops by Premee Mohamed,
Finnian Burnett, and Miranda Krogstad
* Our fabulous "First-page Slush Pile" contest
* Open mic night hosted by Andrew Buckley

Sunday, September 28:
Members brunch at LOCAL Public Eatery

Book your spot today at
wcwfestival.com

Carleigh Baker

Dr. Finnian Burnett

Miranda Krogstad

Premee Mohamed

Do you have a **story to tell?**
We can help!

Dreamers is dedicated to heartfelt writing. Visit our site for:

- Therapeutic Writing
- Poems & Stories
- Content Marketing
- Creative Nonfiction
- Writing Workshops
- Contests & Anthologies
- Residencies & Retreats
- ...and so much more!

www.DreamersWriting.com

Get on board with *Bookworm* for your *free* weekly dose of exclusive reviews, book excerpts, and much more.

Visit *reviewcanada.ca/TTC* or scan the code to the right.

Literary Review of Canada

A JOURNAL OF IDEAS

IGNITE YOUR IMAGINATION

30 yrs of award-winning sci-fi and fantasy

WWW.ONSPEC.CA

THE MAGICAL CONCLUSION TO
THE MUST-READ EPIC TRILOGY

the adventures of Allaigna sing

simply a joy to read

keeps you turning pages from beginning to end

an immensely satisfying epic

PULPLITERATURE.COM/ALLAIGNAS-SONG/

MARKETPLACE

Magazines

Amazing Stories • Back in print!
amazingstories.com

Arc Poetry Magazine • Poetry, essays,
interviews, reviews • arcpoetry.ca

EVENT Magazine • Poetry & prose
eventmagazine.ca

Fiddlehead & SCL • Poetry, fiction,
non-fiction
https://thefiddlehead.ca/

Geist • Ideas + Culture • Made in
Canada • geist.com

Literary Review of Canada • Reviews
on everything from policy and politics
to history, biography, and fiction
https://reviewcanada.ca

Malahat Review • Poetry, fiction,
creative non-fiction
www.malahatreview.ca

OnSpec • The Canadian magazine of
the fantastic
onspecmag.wordpress.com

Polar Borealis • Paying market for
new Canadian SF&F writers & artists
polarborealis.ca

Prairie Fire • A Canadian magazine
of new writing • prairiefire.ca

Room Magazine • Literature, Art &
Feminism since 1975
roommagazine.com

Spadina Literary Review • An international quarterly based in Toronto
spadinaliteraryreview.com

SubTerrain Magazine • Fiction,
poetry, photography, and graphic
illustration from uprising Canadian,
US, and International writers and
artists • https://www.subterrain.ca/

Writing Resources

Dreamers Creative Writing
Workshops • residencies • contests &
more • www.dreamerswriting.com

Federation of BC Writers
Workshops • contests • networking &
more • www.bcwriters.ca/join-us

Printing & Publishing

Fraser Printers • Surrey's Quality
Printer • fraserprinters.bc.ca

CONTESTS

Pulp Literature runs six annual contests for poetry, flash fiction, short stories, and novel first pages. For contest guidelines, prizes, and entry fees, see pulpliterature.com/contests.

The Hummingbird Flash Fiction Prize

Contest opens: 1 May 2025
Deadline: 15 June 2025
Winner notified: 15 July 2025
Winner published: Issue 49, Winter 2026
Prize: $300

The Kingfisher Poetry Prize

Contest opens: 1 July 2025
Deadline: 15 August 2025
Winner notified: 15 September 2025
Winner published: Issue 49, Winter 2026
Prize: $300

The First Page Cage

Contest opens: 1 August 2025
Deadline: 15 September 2025
Winner notified: 15 October 2025
Quarter-finalists published online: Autumn 2025
Prize: $300

The Raven Short Story Contest

Contest opens: 1 September 2025
Deadline: 15 October 2025
Winner notified: 15 November 2025
Winner published: Issue 50, Spring 2026
Prize: $300

The Bumblebee Flash Fiction Contest

Contest opens: 1 January 2026
Deadline: 15 February 2026
Winner notified: 15 March 2026
Winner published: Issue 51, Summer 2026
Prize: $300

The Magpie Award for Poetry

Contest opens: 1 March 2026
Deadline: 15 April 2026
Winner notified: 15 May 2026
Winner published: Issue 52, Autumn 2026
Prize: $500

FICTION • POETRY • COMMENTARY • ART • BOOK REVIEWS
subTerrain
MAGAZINE
SUBSCRIBE NOW!
"It's a damn awesome magazine."
— MIKE CHRISTIE, AUTHOR OF THE BEGGAR'S GARDEN
6 ISSUES ONLY $25
Buy a subscription now and send a FREE one-year subscription to a friend anywhere in North America!
subTerrain.ca/gifts
FOLLOW SUBTERRAIN

FOR
EXPERIMENTAL
WRITING

Submissions August 1-October 15, 2025

First Place = $1000
Second Place = $750
Third Place = $500

All winning pieces will be published in the
Spring 2026 issue of *Grain*.

GRAINMAGAZINE.CA

Cheryl & Henry
Kloppenburg Foundation

2025 Media Kit

Ad Rates

Single Issue

Full page: $250
Half page: $200
Quarter page: $100
Directory (3 text lines): $25

Four Issues

Full page: $795
Half page: $495
Quarter page: $375
Directory (3 text lines): $80

Ad Rates Weekly Digital Newsletter

Our digital weekly newsletter reaches an engaged audience of 2,000 subscribers. With a 54% open rate, our readers consistently interact with and trust the stories, tips, and insights we share.

One Newsletter: $40 | Two Newsletters: $70 | Three Newsletters: $90

Advertise With Us

Full and half-page ads in our quarterly print come with a free directory listing to maximizie your visibility.

To book your ad or learn more, send us an email: info@pulpliterature.com or visit our website at: https://pulpliterature.com/advertise/

Spin the tale only you can tell.

The FIDDLEHEAD
Atlantic Canada's International Literary Journal

ENTER OUR 2025 FICTION CONTEST
OPENS: JUNE 1 | DEADLINE: SEPT. 1, 2025
Enter via Submittable

JUDGED BY:
ANUJA
VARGHESE

$2000 Prize!

+ PLUS PUBLICATION

VISIT: HTTPS://THEFIDDLEHEAD.CA/FICTION-CONTEST

/TheFiddlehead | @fiddlehd.bsky.social | fiddlehd@unb.ca

Become a Patron of *Pulp Literature*

By supporting *Pulp Literature* on Patreon with $2 or more per month, you will be laying the foundation for a secure future for the magazine, as well as ensuring that you never miss an issue! Your subscription includes four big issues of short stories, novellas, poetry, comics, and novel excerpts, delivered to your door or electronic mailbox each year. Find us at **patreon.com/pulplit**.

If you prefer to subscribe through our website, go to pulpliterature. com/subscribe.

Or you can send a cheque with the form below to
Subscriptions, Pulp Literature Press, 21955 16 Ave, Langley BC, V2Z 1K5, Canada

- ❑ **Send me 2 years (8 issues) at the special rate of $110** (save $34)*
- ❑ **Send me 1 year (4 issues) for $60** (save $12)*
- ❑ **Send me 2 years of digital issues for $35** (save $12.92)
- ❑ **Send me 1 year of digital issues for $20** (save $3.96)

Name: ____

Address: ____

City: _______________________________ Prov. / State: _________

Postal code: ______________ Country: ___________________

Email: ____

- ❑ **Payment enclosed**
- ❑ **Bill me**
- ❑ **New**
- ❑ **Renewal**

Make cheques payable in Canadian funds to Pulp Literature Press. Include email address for digital editions and Paypal billing, or subscribe at www.pulpliterature.com/subscribe.

*for postage outside Canada add $20 per year in North America or $32 per year overseas.